1

Marginal Waters:
The Brat Chronicles

published by Fiesta Creative Arts

printed in United States by CreateSpace

a division of Amazon

ISBN-13:

978-1984306746

to order visit amazon.com or

Barnes and Noble

Text, layout and editing by

R. Rundle

ronrundle@gmail.com

Raccoons knitted by Penny Rundle

Other Titles by R. Rundle

Elementary Grades

Miss Angela (gr. 4-6)

The Walker Boys (gr. 4-6)

The Dark Side of the Moon (gr. 7 & 8)

Adventures in Babysitting (gr. 5-8)

Adventures in Babysitting: I Have a Dark Passenger (gr. 6-8)

This is New (gr.7 & 8)

Just an Ordinary Joe (gr. 8)

Pearl (gr. 8)

Rocket Girl (gr. 8)

There's a New Girl in Town (gr. 7-8)

Marginal Waters: Monster's Edition (gr. 6-8)

The Brat Chronicles (gr. 6-8)

Dragon (gr. 6-8)

Wherever I Go (gr. & up)

A Passing Ship (gr. 8 & up)

High School

Starfinder

High School & Adult

Marginal Waters

Marginal Waters: The After Party

Marginal Waters: The Invasion of the Woodpeckers

Marginal Waters: I Have a Dark Passenger

Prologue

If you got to the fifth book in the series you are familiar with the kinds of characters that seem to be attracted to Marginal Waters. Some are relatively normal, others have arrived in need of sanctuary and restoration as mentioned in 'I Have a Dark Passenger'. Some in spite of the therapeutic effects of Marginal Waters manage to remain broken. I have to admit I find this sub culture annoying and will just leave it at that. Actually of the most of the inmates are just fine, using Marginal Waters as a weekend sanctuary, a place to kick back, relax, cook a burg, and maybe do a little howling at the moon. There is definitely something about he place because once most of the characters arrive, most of them stay.

This book in part deals with some of the 'brats' of Marginal Waters i.e. the offspring of the adult members of the community. What do you suppose they would be like? Well we have the apple and tree theory, so the kids will likely be to some degree a reflection of their parents, as children generally learn was they are taught. They become a blend of their parents plus influences outside the home. Those of you that have children know it can be a bit of a mine field. My own personal theory for what it's worth, love them unconditionally, model the behaviour you want, then insure everything and hope for the best.

You have briefly met a few Marginal Waters children already, A.D.H.D. Mary, who initially was more than a bit of a pain but is now doing well, her boundless energy burned off to some degree by her work with the Happy Gang. Leah and Eddy are growing up well, with only minor issues but to date not too many of the children have been talked about, until now.

The child population of Marginal Waters is a little on the light side, perhaps for the best because some of the residents seem to have difficulty looking after themselves. The skid row geezers are almost too old to have functioning reproductive parts, so many of the new kids are fairly recent migrants, drawn in with their parents.

Since the atmosphere is pretty much live and let live, Marginal Waters is a secure environment, and their parents realize it so children pretty much can move about freely. Really small children are generally well supervised but as children age, they tend to grow a leash, getting longer and longer the older they get, often testing its strength against their parents, many secretly and some not so secretly wanting the leash to snap.

Freedom and adventure, young humans crave it, perhaps we all do, I believe it is our nature because, what's life without adventure. But most parents are not really interested in their children's lives being filled with too much adventure, but that wish seldom stops them.

The first case is an example of an early unwilling member of the community, drawn in with resistance by her parents.

We Bought a What?

Emma waved her hand back and forth in the air like she was hailing a cab, hoping to get her teacher's attention; it wasn't working. She thought briefly about snapping her fingers; she only tried that once and it wasn't well received and it was suggested she not do that again. She knew Mrs. Marshall had a sense of humour but she had discovered not about that. Finally after much waving her teacher looked at her and said with a slightly tired sigh,

"What's the problem Emma?" She pointed.

"That friggen clock is dead!" After a full year she knew this young girl well but even at the end of the year, and ready for a break from the class of restless hormone filled adolescents before her, still had a smile and said patiently.

"Sorry it's two o'clock, one more hour," and still being the teacher advised, "Another adjective other than friggin would be more ladylike." Emma whimpered and put her head down on top of her hands, muttering into her desk top.

"Time has stopped, the year will never end." She sat up and touched the back of her hand to her forehead. "I feel faint, I think I may swoon." She looked around with the back of her hand still against her forehead, and one arm extended.

"Pray for me classmates." Her teacher had to put her hand over here mouth to hide the laugh; her classmates just rolled their eyes. One of her best friends just called out.

"Emmy, shut up!" Often the drama queen she remembered her mother using the swoon comment when she was getting stressed out, usually from Emma, who if you haven't figured it out yet is a little bit of a restless pain. Her along with the rest of the 'chickens' had been in the coup long enough; it was time as many bartenders have said at closing.

"You don't have to go home but you can't stay here."

Finally the most joyous sound, the end of the year bell. She was out of her chair like a rocket, out the door and down the street at full throttle, bursting though the back door, kicked off her shoes and slid across the smooth floor, arms extended yelling,

"Stop makin' out, I'm home!"

Her mother and father had news and we're pretty sure daughter number one and only would have some issues about it. They were sitting at the kitchen table being fortified for the task with an afternoon whiskey. This usually meant there was some kind of issue to deal with and daughter was generally at the centre of it. Her dad smiled at her.

"So that's it for grade eight." She rubbed her hands together and gave her parents an evil grin.

"Yep you got me for the whole summer, got some money for booze and dope? Now that I'm headed for high school, got to get in shape." They exchanged glances and took a sip and her dad rolling his eyes only slightly; he had heard stuff like this from his daughter before.

"Emmy, take a seat." She was starting to suspect something was going on and looked from one to another.

"S'up parents?" Her mother took a sip of the whiskey of her own.

"Just sit and take a breath dear." Emma knew this was serious; she was hoping nobody was sick or something, oddly a bit of a fatalist even at thirteen.

"Just tell me." Her dad gave her the news.

"We bought a boat." Emma leaned her elbows on the table and put her chin on the back of her folded hands, one of several poses she used when being dramatic, though that news didn't seem too bad. However, she suspected there was more to this story, and asked.

“Is that all?” Her mom took another sip causing Emma to look at her imaginary wristwatch and raise her eyebrows. A slightly accusatory but silent comment on her mother’s afternoon drinking. Don’t kids like the view from the high ground when they realize their parents have feet of clay. Her mother slipped a picture of the boat across to her.

“There it is.” She noticed immediately there was a young girl standing on the dock in front of it. She was initially impressed.

“Wow, big!” Her father buoyed by her initial positive impression gave her the really big news.

“We’re going to live on it this summer, something new.” Now this triggered several questions from a girl often full of questions.

“Not here at all?” Her mother took another sip and delivered what she knew would not be well received.

“No.” Emma leaned closer.

“So…” She dragged it out, “no soccer, summer camp, hanging with my buds?” Her dad picked up his side of the script.

“No, they’ll be other things to do, you’ll see.” This was not at all good news for an urban kid with the summer ahead of her, all planned and currently lots to do and lots of friends. She had activities that did not include living away from her own digs and hangouts in a smaller container than her house and room. She simply bolted upstairs to her room and slammed the door, leaving her parents to sip their whiskey and formulate plan 'B'. Her dad patted his wife's hand gently.

"Let's let her majesty cool down for a couple of minutes." Her mom smiled and shook her head slightly as she looked upstairs towards her daughter's room.

"Did you ever think maybe we just should have stayed with a cat, less trouble, significantly quieter." They gave each other a knowing look, but that ship had indeed sailed; her majesty was of course a permanent fixture.

Her dad gave her a few minutes then left the whiskey behind and went upstairs tapping on her door.

"Emmy, can I come in?" There was a muffled.

"Sure, as long as you're not going to tell me I'm getting a baby brother." Her dad put his hand over his mouth so as not to laugh, thinking, one little lunatic is more than enough. He walked in and sat down on the bed. Herself, another name as she was called when she was being a pain was laying on her bed face down with her pillow piled on top of her head. It was a teenage episode of my life is over, again. For her Dad it was time to get mildly stern.

"Ok, turn over and sit up." Slowly she emerged from under her pillow, rolled over and sat up, the face appearing from under her pile of long hair. She gave her dad the sad little girl doe eyes which he ignored. They sat together for a minute, finally he said,

"Listen it's not even close to the end of the world, so start packing light for summer, be a little more positive and look at it as a new experience, no more pouting or complaining, got it?" Emma shrugged.

"Yeah, got it, don't have any choice do I?" Her dad nodded.

"Nope, but look at the bright side, you get to keep living as part of this loving family," he put a little emphasis on the word loving, "three squares, everything you need and most of what you want." He put his arm around her shoulder.

"Remember, loved," then kissed her on top of the head, " very dearly." She looked at him and leaned her head against his shoulder; she had short snap count but cooled down quickly and also knew but needed to be reminded that what he said was true.

"Love you dad, I'll get my stuff together, when we leaving?" Her dad got up, ready to head back and finish the rest of his whiskey, but glad the issue was settled, for now. He smiled as he headed out the door.

"We're leaving Tuesday morning." She called out.

"Where we going anyway?" He called back.

"It's a marina up north called Marginal Waters." She called to him as he headed down the stairs.

"Sounds a little sketchy." Her dad yelled back at her.

"You'll fit right in then." All her heard was a scolding.

"Daddy!"

So Long Pops

Sam stood with the rest of the gathered relatives and a few other people he didn't know at the local cemetery, feeling like the consummate stranger in a strange land. He was looking around thinking, nice day, be better to be at the old ball yard scooping up some grounders, but as his dad said, always a way with words.

"Could be worse, could be raining." However this was one of those things that his dad also called a command performance. Sam hooked one finger inside his shirt collar and tugged; his tie seemed to be ratcheting itself tighter around his neck as the afternoon wore on. He wondered why men would wear one of these things on purpose.

This was his first funeral; knew they happened of course but one of the many plusses about being thirteen was his family and of course friends were on the young side, fortunately he'd never had the experience. But it's part of growing up, realizing that we are not immortal, everything dies. Still being his first funeral, the whole experience seemed just plain strange and mildly disturbing. You'll never really get used to it by the way, hope you don't have to attend too many of them. I think it probably reminds us that one day we'll be the centre of attention.

There were words being spoken Sam simply did not understand. He did wonder what the Holy Ghost looked like and where hell he was. Perhaps he was at the old ball yard working on his swing. Reminded of that he took a pretend swing with an imaginary bat and muttered to himself.

"Watch the ball, head down, quick bat, quick bat." That got a small look from his dad, so it was hands back to the sides and back to the present rather than his imaginary at bat. What he did know was where his Pops was, well he assumed he was in still in the very shiny box that was about to be lowered into the ground, forever.

He then heard what he figured was the closing phrase.

"Here's to the Father, Son and Holy Ghost." He had been daydreaming a bit and thought he heard something odd. He whispered to his Dad.

"What did he say?" His father had been daydreaming as well but not as much as Sam, whispered back.

"The Father, Son and Holy Ghost." Sam whispered back.

"I thought he said, 'The Father, Son and into the hole he goes." Sam's dad and he had the same sense of humour and this struck him as beyond funny. He had to clamp his lips together so he wouldn't laugh. Sam looked up at his Dad who was holding a laugh in so hard he was shaking. His dad finally whispered back.

"The Holy Ghost Sammy, not into the hole he goes." Sam whispered back.

"What's the Holy Ghost look like?" His dad clamped his mouth closed again but whispered back.

"Sammy, shut up." Then they both heard a whisper from guess who?"

"If you two clowns don't put a sock in it there's going to be a serious beat down!" They both straightened up and whispered.

"Sorry dear."

"Sorry mom." But still had a hard time stifling a laugh. They managed to stand quietly for the rest of the service. Sam figured maybe he should do some serious thinking about Pops; the man was dead.

He knew he was supposed to feel bad but for a few reasons couldn't come up with the that emotion. One was his substitute grandfather or Pops as he was required to call him and he were never very close. When he thought about it Pops never seemed close to anyone. Sam always found him a little on the grouchy side and seemed to be constantly sipping from a shiny silver container that he now knew contained whiskey. Also as he looked around, none of the assembled relatives and friends seemed to be very upset either some were just looking around, some glancing at their phones. He was guessing like him were all wishing they were somewhere else. He wondered what the whole point was but came to no conclusion other than it seemed like an elaborate and probably expensive disposal system.

When it was over, and father and son had calmed down his dad came over to him.

"You ok son?"

"I'm good dad," and in a moment of personal growth thinking I'm not in the ground like good old Pops. His dad then gave him some very unexpected information.

"We're going from here to the will reading." Sam looked up, very surprised.

"We?" Sam figured his work was done after this; the tie was going in the harbour, and the suit on the hanger. It would be fine if he never had to go to another funeral in his life. His dad put his hand on his shoulder.

"We got a list of the people that are expected to attend and you're the only one on it; we're going cause you need a drive." He stared at his Dad, completely amazed.

"Me!" His dad just nodded. For Sam that was an absolute surprise, figuring his work was done, but thought, maybe good old Pops was a secret multi-millionaire and he was going to inherit a vineyard in Spain and a fleet of racing cars, maybe a jet, he thought, I could have my own stewardess. A fairly imaginative young man already influenced by mother nature was having a moment constructing his imaginary life as a multi-millionaire complete with a stewardess for his jet, or maybe a girl pilot as well. Yes he mused two blondes I think, both with long legs and beautiful smiles. We could fly to baseball games, I could sit between them in the owner's box. He was brought out of this spectacular daydream when the car door shut with a dull thunk. Back to reality, stuck in the back seat with good old dad driving the family car not his own piloted Gulfstream wide body executive jet.

The drive to the lawyer's office with his parents was a quiet one; it again seemed to Sam that no one really cared that Pops was dead, including his parents. His mom and dad chatted quietly; he knew it was about Pops, but so quietly it was difficult to eavesdrop. He heard his mom whisper.

"Can you believe there's no gathering after?" His dad who always made his point succinctly said,

"We care as much as he did." His mom turned around, as usual in constant concern about Sam's well being asked.

"You sure you're ok Sam?" Sam just shrugged.

"I'm good mom, know anything about this will?" She reached and patted his hand.

"Nothing." Sam however could read the expression on his mother's face and a slight tone in her voice; he knew she was not part of the Pops fan club.

The whole family's view of Pops was the same, partly because over most of his life he was fairly reclusive, often disappearing for months at a time. When he was around and in family gatherings he often migrated to a distant chair to be by himself and sip his whiskey. His body language never encouraged conversation. Word was he started out as a young man living alone, eventually migrating to Sam's grandmother's place because the food was always good.

Sam knew him from family gatherings and he also hung around Marginal Waters the same marina as his parents; he came and went, spent a fair amount of time fiddling with his boat. He would take it out quite often with a passenger much younger than himself. He would peg the throttle roaring around the lake for about a half an hour, then pack up and disappear with his passenger in his way cool Maserati convertible. One of the other things about him that was mysterious, in spite of the fact that he was approaching geezerhood, his companions always seemed to remain young.

His boat was another story, and much more atheistic than Pops. Sitting still it was quite the craft, about ten meters long but only two seats, near the back. The rest was set aside for a long shiny deck with a huge antique engine under it; it looked something like a mahogany cigar. Running it had a deep rumbling growl, a bit smoky and uncivilized from its aging engine. Sam was told the engine was originally designed for some classic warplane.

There was much speculation from the boat's name that Pops assembled his wealth from running controlled substances to various locations, hence the name Baby Bootlegger, but they like many of the ideas about Pops were just speculation. One thing that was true the passenger seat on Baby Bootlegger was becoming less and less occupied as Pops got older.

Sam would find very soon that people are seldom what they seem, they are either less or more. Pops definitely had a back story, actually many of them. He didn't realize it but soon he was going to be drawn into these stories.

Sam always did like the boat though; the name seemed to suit it, when Pops fired it up it snarled and smoked, while it warmed up, kind of like an untrained guard dog that had just been woken up from his nap, somewhat bad tempered like its owner. Can machines take on the personality of their owner? However, all warmed up skimming across the water it was in its element and a thing of beauty, lots of shiny wood and sparkling chrome two sprays of water and a nice deep throaty growl from its side exhausts. There was a brutal elegance to it especially if you like to go fast and make lots of noise.

It might have occurred to you how can you have a grandfather without a Mrs. Pops. Well there's another Pops mystery, he was sort of adopted by Sam's grandmother who lost her husband at a young age. There was some quiet discussion in the family as to how close Pops was to Sam's grandmother but in Sam's grandmother's generation, such topics were deemed personal business, meaning it was personal and nobody's business. She never talked about their relationship and the family had the good sense not to ask.

That philosophy seems to have disappeared lately, as every thought, muse, feeling, deed and relationship is photographed, shared, posted, tweeted, Facebooked and texted about extensively. And as always there was good old gossip as the sharing about every detail of everybody's life seems endless.

With the short drive over Sam and his family gathered in the lawyer's office. Sam was impressed, the lawyer was seated behind a desk about three metres long with a huge picture window overlooking the harbour. This Sam correctly figured this was not cheap working digs. As an added bonus a very attractive secretary came and asked,

"Would anyone like anything, coffee, tea, soft drink?" She gave Sam a big smile, figuring Sam was an innocent with regard to girls and women; he was not as mother nature had been working on him for a few months. Sam thought, sweetheart you could be a stewardess on my imaginary jet. Sam smiled back, occasionally an amateur comedian.

"Two fingers, Jack, up." He smiled at the secretary again and flipped up his thumb. Those of you not familiar with the lingo of alcohol, that means two ounces of Jack Daniels whiskey (an American derivative of actual whiskey, I won't start), up means straight, no ice. Sam's dad rolled his eyes, thinking a shot of Jack for himself might hit the spot right now and excused his smart assed son.

"We have decided to find Sam's sense of humour charming." Sam figured it was time to stop and gave the secretary his gentlemanly smile and polite reply.

"Thank you, I'm good." He had also discovered that if you were polite, humorous and not obnoxious with women sometimes you got a little touch on the arm or pat on the back, and if they found you extra cute, a kiss on the cheek He liked all that, but all he got was a smile as his imaginary stewardess likely disappeared out of his life forever. He sighed and turned around; again it was back to his teenage reality.

He looked around perplexed, other than him and his parents there was nobody else. He figured correctly that Pops had no other family but why Sam's grandmother did not attend would be really good question. Sam guessed she was not in the will, that would tick her and the rest of the family off since Pops lived with her, on and off that is for as long as Sam could remember. Some of the family really looked down at this calling Pops a raccoon, feeding and bedding down in a comfortable spot. Note: I will discuss the issue of raccoons, i.e. four and two legged versions in a later chapters, for now, moving on.

Sam's parents were even more mystified than Sam. Pops was truly a combination of an enigma, black sheep and a conundrum all rolled into one, but they figured the will would be simple, even though he drifted in and out of the grandmother's life, whatever he had would be left to her. Why it apparently wasn't and why he insisted that Sam and only Sam be there was a complete mystery.

They all listened with extreme interest as the lawyer started.

"Good afternoon everyone, I'm Bernard Reilly by the way, welcome Mr. and Mrs. Clarkson, and of course Sam. I'll read the will as written, and by the way, this is most of what I was given." That was a carefully crafted sentence that nobody picked up on.

Hello Sam,

Your Pops here, if you are hearing this I'm dead, so my stuff is of no use to me. I'm leaving you 'Baby Bootlegger'; it's at the marina, probably a little dusty and in need of some TLC. It was built in the 1920's; I've had it for a few years and now she's yours. It has an upgraded Hispano-Suiza HS-12Y engine. I know that means nothing to you but it is an antique but kick ass motor. I think it will still run; you want to hope it doesn't need any parts. There's a drum of 100 octane aviation gas at the marina, don't be putting the usual marina pump gas swill in it, won't run worth beans.

You are probably wondering why, well I know we didn't know each other very well but I liked you, you're smart and I've actually seen you working on a boat or two, could be because you've got a little thing for Mary but we all get a little thing for some girl. Isn't she as cute as a rabbit wearing a hat.

By the way the rest of the will is on 'Baby Bootlegger', as you clean it up or poke around you will find it in various places and in pieces. What you do with it and the boat for that matter is up to you. A final note, storage has been paid for three years so, that gives you time. A little advice if I may, son, value your time, there's only so much, make it count. As you know, mine's run out.

Good sailing and good luck

Pops (James) MacFarlin

Mr. Reilly put the will down and took off his glasses. Sam and his parents waited for something else as the room descended into silence. Finally Mr. Reilly said,

"That's it, that's all there is to the will. I must say I've been in this business for some time, never seen a will like that. Sounds like there's more but you have to find it." He stood up. "Mr. and Mrs. Clarkson, could I have a word with Sam alone?" They both nodded, figuring Sam would be alright for a bit and left. After the door closed he said,

"Sam just sit for a minute, there's a little more." Sam just sat there waiting. "You're most likely going to get more information, can't say how, because I don't know. What I do know is there's money, lots, but it's complicated and I can't say any more than that. Pops paid me well and a lawyer is only as good as his loyalty to his client, so you're on your own here." He reached out his hand. "Good luck." Sam had been temporarily distracted when he heard money picturing himself in Pop's Maserati on the way to the airport, his imaginary stewards back in his life. He snapped out of it.

"Ok sir, thanks, I guess." When he got outside the office his mom asked.

"What was that about." Sam just shook his head and said honestly.

"I'm not sure." His dad gave him a pat on the back.

"Well looks like you'll have something to do at the marina this summer."

Baby Bootlegger

Sam sat crosslegged on the dock surveying his new boat, even though it was early summer and all the boats were in the water, there she sat blocked in one of the work slips sitting on three massive Douglas Fir beams. It had not been launched because Pops had died before it was ready to go in. It was next to the Happy Gang's shop and hangout, where Sam's beloved Mary worked. Sam looked over a copy of the will that was left for him; he'd read it a dozen times. Other than the boat itself, there didn't appear to be anything else specifically mentioned. There was nothing about money in the will or his snazzy red Maserati that Sam really would have liked. The will was basically an invitation to have a closer look at Baby Bootlegger to look for more details. Would it be another document or Sam thought, maybe a wad of cash and the keys to the red Maserati, but that was all just speculation. He really had no idea what to do and said out loud.

"Well she's quite the beast but what am I supposed to do with this thing?" And like magic the sawdust garnished angel appeared and sat down beside him. My god Sam thought, that smile just digs right inside me.

“Well clean it up for a start.” It was Mary, to date his only true but still secret love. She gave him a little punch on the shoulder to bring him out of his worship trance. “Hey Sam.” Sam blushed instantly and managed only to get out.

“Mary.” He hadn’t seen her yet this spring and he noticed immediately somehow she had gotten more beautiful over the winter. As usual she didn’t even have to try at all, cut off tatty old blue jeans and a work ’T’ shirt with varnish and paint stains, her pile of multi-coloured auburn hair gathered in a sort of pony tail that seemed to explode out of the top of her head. She often had a couple of little sawdust shavings in he hair that he always wanted to pick out but never did. He had thought on many occasions the most beautiful girl he had ever seen in real life. However there were a couple of problems in the way of true romance, one she was seventeen and he was thirteen, so not likely, but on the bright side Sam had never seen her with a boyfriend, so she was available. But, leading to problem two, other than the occasional punch on the shoulder she had shown no romantic interest in Sam. And actually Mary currently had no romantic interest in anyone, and viewed Sam as a likeable adolescent boy and that was it. She smiled and stood up.

"Got to get to work, Jack and Charlie are going to drop around," she reached over and ran her hand over Baby Bootlegger's transom, "and have a look at the old girl."

Mary had been drawn into the Order of the Woodpecker; she had developed an unexplainable affection for old boats and varnished wood. Maybe the varnish fumes are some kind of permanent mood altering narcotic, but it's a matter of art, so nobody know for sure other than art is not easy.

Not exactly sure how it happens myself, been in the Order for a long time and the affection or affliction depending on your attitude appears to be terminal. Sam thought and blushed as he watched her long slender fingers slide off the corner of the transom with what appeared to be some kind of affection. He was thinking, I wish she'd run her hand over me like that. She brought him out of his teenage romantic/erotic fantasy as she gave him another punch.

"And this is Emma, she's new to the marina, so be nice. Emma this is Sam." Emma was left feeling a little awkward realized immediately she was running a distant second to Mary as she watched Sam stare at Mary's butt as she walked away. Emma rolled her eyes and tapped her foot, wondering if boys were all the same, but determined not to be ignored completely she sat down beside him and whispered.

"Psst, girl on your left." Sam turned and blushed, caught in the act, but snapped out of it as his fantasy goddess disappeared up the stairs into the restoration shop. He finally got out an embarrassed,

"Hey." Emma figured she'd have a little fun.

"So where would you rate her butt, one to ten?" Sam blushed hopelessly.

"I wasn't looking at that." Emma nodded and smiled.

"Sure Sam, whatever you say." Having a longer awkward moment they sat each wondering what to say to the other. Finally Emma figured she should say something not butt related.

"I hear that's your boat?" He nodded glad the conversation had moved on.

"Yep, somebody left it to me, and it would be a good question what I'm supposed to do with it."

For Emma what to do with the whole place was a good question. It was a completely new and strange environment. Lot's of neighbours with their boats so close to each other you could spit and hit them. To the right of her boat was somebody that was called Robert the Mutant. She wondered what the mutation was but he appeared harmless. He kept to himself for the most part and you could always hear the quiet hum of a palm sander, the faint odour of varnish and paint thinner, all accompanied by Gordon Lightfoot tunes. She didn't know much about him other than he had an old boat which he seemed to work on endlessly, gathered at the end of the day and in the evening with a few of his whiskey drinking buddies and surprisedly she heard he was a ringer in barrel beer pong, whatever that was. She viewed him as pleasant but noted, older than dirt, so, you know. To her right was a younger couple with two annoying dogs, she guessed were substitutes for children. Emma was not really a dog person and the dogs seemed to know that. They yapped at her whenever she wandered by and on more than one occasion she thought I could put a tight spiral on both those useless mutts and toss them right in the middle of the harbour.

However the harbour currently would not be a good place for her as she couldn't even swim though her dad had already enrolled her in swimming lessons. She was indeed a stranger in the strange land called Marginal Waters, an urban dry land girl occasionally getting wet in the shallow end of her buddy Marci's pool. Now she was living at the water's edge, mere feet from certain death if she fell in on a 'house' that moved when you stepped on it.

She had been living on their boat for only two days and though she had her own cabin found it a little claustrophobic. She hadn't met anyone her age until now and wasn't instantly too impressed with Sam. All her old friends and activities had been left behind, replaced by who knows what. However one of the many plusses of her personality was an innate curiosity and lots of confidence. She figured she was here, may as well draw the bat back and swing.

"Going to check it out," And climbed the small ladder that was leaning against the hull side of Baby Bootlegger and looked in the cockpit.

"Can I get in?" Sam shrugged showing his limited interest. She climbed in nestling down into the quite comfortable leather captain's chair and put her hands on the steering wheel.

"Kind of cool in here, even the wheel is made out of wood." She looked around, "how do you make it go, no gas pedal?" Sam had not even climbed in yet and climbed the ladder looking in

"Its got a throttle lever, on your right." She reached up and fiddled with it.

"Cool, what's the other lever?." Sam said with authority.

"Transmission shifter, forward, neutral, reverse." She nodded and looked at the floor.

"No brakes." Sam laughed at this new land lubber.

"They don't have brakes, just reverse to slow down." She smiled.

"Good to know." She was picturing herself at the wheel cruising around the lake, sunglasses and a jaunty hat.

Surprisingly it was not too dirty inside the cockpit as Sam had just recently pulled off the snapped down cover. He jumped in beside her, both realizing they were in each other's personal space. Emma noted,

"You don't smell too bad for a boy." Sam laughed.

"Well that's a ringing endorsement." She stood up looking down the long deck. "Looks like a big wooden cigar." Sam nodded.

"It's called a Gold Cup Racer, built in 1920, wait, take a look at the engine." Like most men enjoying his new found role as expert. Sam flicked a switch and two huge engine hatches slowly opened. The hydraulic rams to control the hatches were installed by Tom when Pops got too old to lift them manually. Emma leaned over.

“Wow! The engine was indeed huge, about two metres long and a meter high and almost as old as the boat, with lots of brass tubes and pipes running everywhere. Emma was actually getting excited.

“I bet it’s fast.” Sam agreed.

“Supposed to do close to a hundred miles an hour, however fast that is.” Sam being a modern kid had no knowledge of this former measure of speed. Emma being better with numbers said,

“One hundred and sixty kph.” Sam’s eyes widened.

“That might be fun.” Emma was getting into it and climbed over the deck in with the engine. She looked under the deck

“What’s in here?” Sam just shrugged and to his surprise she disappeared into the inside of the hull, not too tall and nimble she could crawl around easily. Sam called in after her.

“What’s in there?” He could hear her crawling forward.

"Not much, wood," a little pause, "more wood, dust getting dark, yuck, spider, spider, yuck coming out!" He could hear her crawling back a little faster, "more dust, hang on, found something." Then to his surprise she came out with a book.

"What's this?" Sam had no idea, he hadn't even been inside the boat yet.

She climbed back and put the book on the small dashboard. It looked like a simple three ring binder. She flipped open the cover and inside was a picture of a young woman inside a plastic sheet cover; she flipped the next page, same thing, another one. Over and over again, there were about ten pictures in the book of different women. As they got to the last picture. It was Sam's grandmother as a younger woman. Sam picked up the book and blew some dust off it, then gently wiped the dust off the last page.

"This last picture is my grandmother, younger picture." Emma looked.

"She's beautiful." Sam smiled having a great affection for his grandmother.

"Still is, she thinks I'm wonderful." Emma teased.

"Imagine that, " and began flipping back through the pages.

"Some of these pictures are old." She was getting a little excited. "There's more to this than a boat." Being a girl and also smart, the pictures in the book were obvious. "These women were important for whoever owned this boat." Sam handed her the letter. She read it carefully then closed it up.

"You've got to get into all this." Always loving a mystery added. "I'll help, got nothing to do this summer, except learn to swim." Jack and Charlie had arrived and were standing behind the kids just listening. Sam thought he'd be friendly, and he had noticed a couple of things.

"I can swim I'll teach you, there's a little beach at the end of the marina." Mother nature had for sure been working on Sam; Emma was not Mary but at thirteen she was his age and he had noticed quite easy on the eyes, long dark hair and big brown eyes, and also the other usual standard equipment that boys notice. He suspected from talking to her, smarter than him, and had been well coached by his mother not to be threatened by a smart girl. She whispered.

"I secretly want to go skinny dipping one day." Sam blushed hopelessly, developing a picture of Emma skinny dipping. He was snapped out of his problem as Charlie spoke from behind him.

"Sammy, hang out with this girl for a few years, then marry her." Charlie being Charlie stepped forward, "Hello miss, I'm Charlie, my buddy Jack, we know a bit about these old girls." Emma smiled.

"I'm Emma sir," then whispered to Sam.

"Why are all boats girls?" Sam thought about her question.

"No idea, they are though." Jack climbed up on the staging planks next to Baby Bootlegger and answered her question.

"Cause men fall in love with them; and they're a lot less complicated than women." He smiled. "Who are nothing but trouble." Emma stuck her tongue out at him causing him to just smile and ignore.

"Let's have a look." The kids sat as Charlie and Jack ran their hands up and down the boat's hull, looking in the open engine hatches. Poor Sam kept glancing at Emma, still surprised by her skinny dipping comment. He whispered,

"You're weird." She gave him a little smile.

"Little bit, but I'm cute." Charlie who was still looking at the boat called out.

"You know she's just messing with you." In the meantime she had crawled back inside the boat and she stuck her head out through the hatch opening.

"No I ain't." Charlie tipped his hat to Emma and said,

"I repeat, Sammy hang with this girl and marry her someday."

Charlie and Jack were finally finished. Jack waved them over to where he was standing.

"Guys, come here." They did as they were told and he ran his hand over the round hull. "Feel this?" Emma did.

"It's got a little spot that's not round." She nodded. That flat spot means there's a broken frame; they're like ribs in your body, provide support. They've got to be fixed, but you've got to take off some planks to get to them. We'll mark the planks that have to be removed." Sam moved in as well not wanting to be left behind by a girl. He asked,

"How do you get the planks off?" Charlie pulled out a small X-acto knife and sliced a wooden plug then carefully pried it out. Charlie pointed,

“There’s the screw, clean around it and carefully turn out the screw, you don’t want to damage the plank. Without the screws they’ll just fall off. Set the them aside; they can be reused. When you get them all off we’ll come back and give you lesson two.” Jack moved in with two X-acto knives and a screwdriver.

“Here the first simple tools of the wooden boat restorer..” He put them in small toolboxes. Charlie pulled out two T shirts.

“And we got you work shirts.” He held them up. On the front it said their names and on the back it said.

“The Order of the Woodpecker.”

The kids were quite taken aback. Emma grabbed hers and put it on holding up her hands and spinning around.

“What do you think?” Charlie nodded and said to Sam who was struggling to get the shirt on.

“Sammy, you got a good deck hand here, I speak from experience, they are hard to find.”

Raccoons

I return to the briefly aforementioned issue of raccoons. Marina people will know about the four legged versions already, but may have not run across the relatively common sub species called Two Legged Raccoons, a term used to describe Sam's grandpa Pops and requires some explanation. Raccoons, both two and four legged ones and I go way back. I have observed both species in action many times.

The most common are four legged raccoons and in my opinion the scourge of home and boat if they get inside your digs. After many encounters this writer who is basically a friend of living things came to a conclusion. The only good raccoon is a dead one! And I really don't care how they die, splattered into chum by a semi, or taken out by a hail of shot gun pellets, don't care as long as they are dead, and therefore, not living in my attic or boat.

I will explain; friends have had them winter on their boats eating everything they can chew, wiring, upholstery, apparently in search of traces of salt left behind on people's furniture. As an added bonus are the only animal I know that will crap and pee in their own nest. Since they are a significantly sized animal can drop their body weight in one dump. Sometimes they even do the dishonour of dying on board not dragging their festering body off the boat to at least expire in the woods; the stink is unbelievable.

I had them move into my attic for a winter, trapped and removed two dozen of them; they kept coming back, not the same raccoon but it is truly is hard to tell, seen one you've seen them all. I swear they are telepathic, somehow sending messages to their friends and relatives to join the party, in my house! Nothing like listening to a constipated one bearing down on a hopeful crap in your attic. Where are the raccoons I removed? Well the answer is similar to the one given in a chapter in the fourth book called Yes We Have No Bananas, don't ask don't tell. Well you are basically filled in the four legged versions.

You might still be wondering how can raccoons be two legged? Well two legged raccoons are people of course but they have many disturbing similarities to their in my view not too distant four legged cousins.

One they will move into somebody else's nest, settle in, eat, bed down and crap. They will stay as long as they are allowed unless in their view a better nest presents itself, then like the more instinctively driven counterpart, simply migrate to a new home.

As an added bonus they contribute next to nothing, either convincing themselves that they are of such significant cultural value to their newly adopted home that their mere presence is enough. Or I think far more clever and devious than they are given credit for, having the ability to sense what nest is the most accessible and perhaps prosperous. I know one personally (two legged of course) and the first thing he checks on a boat is does the fridge work? And I believe just as important, is it full of cold beer and provisions. They realize pretty fast that winter is coming, time to turn on the charm and offer whatever it is they have to offer, except money. Some are pretty good at staying put for years, leaving only when they sense the tide is turning or there is promise of a better nest.

Like the more usual raccoons the two legged variety can come in both male and female by the way; I've known a few personally, seen them in operation. They can also travel in pairs, some linked through blood and others through some kind of realization that they are birds of a feather. In pairs they are often more troublesome. Obviously in pairs they consume more food and beer. I have seen one particular pair waiting to be fed by somebody who has worked all week to buy the food they are going to eat. And another earmark of two legged raccoons; they often don't work at all or some skillfully pretend to work. I call it creating the illusion of labour. They can be seen relaxing at two the afternoon, right in the cusp of a supposed work day. Also in pairs with so much down time they can get together and plot how to entrench themselves even deeper into the fabric of a good nest.

You might ask how does a person drift into the Order of the Raccoon? I theorize several ways; those of you that know me realize I have theories about most everything. Not suggesting they are all correct but I cover myself by once again using Dennis Miller's old line.

"It's just my opinion, I could be wrong." Let the theories begin.

I think some fall into the apple and tree theory; if you are raised by layabouts then you are more likely to continue in that path. I know one set of raccoons that fit that theorem, son is very similar to father.

Some drift into the lifestyle accidentally through job loss and rather than find another one just lay around so long that they can't face getting up and going to work again. Along with that they have parents/friends/lovers who have the means but not will to say.

"Son/daughter/sweetheart I love you but you need a plan to participate in the maintenance of this nest or find your own."

Others, and these are the most scary are really smart and have figured out how it's done on several fronts, sponging off various friends and relatives until the string runs out, if it runs out at all. They are also able to sense when the wind is not blowing with them and can adapt and morph into a more successful raccoon, not only sponging from private sources but have been able to get the state, (that is the rest of us) to fund their lifestyle, such as it is.

I realize in the last paragraph I drift in politics; I won't stay long. The down side of a prosperous left leaning democracy is the formation of what I call the Nanny State. People of the Order of the Raccoon are actually funded to be lazy, or fertile or stay psychologically broken, or some or all of the above. Also consuming state funded (again, that's us) therapy, drugs, food and shelter. Also on the other down side, also as mentioned they are often remarkable fertile and tend to proliferate, spreading spawn similar to themselves, following the apple tree theory, creating more problem makers than problem solvers from a shallow gene pool, that get's shallower over time. A good friend of mine correctly said.

"You don't breed quarter horses and get Kentucky Derby winners" The numbers of problem maker population is growing and a good question is how many of them can the rest of us support before the whole system just runs out of money?

Well to sum up the real question is what to do about it. On the state level the only way seems to be what happened in western Europe in the last few months. Indolent party going nations with herds of raccoons simply ran out of money. On a personal level, two legged raccoons in my opinion can be dealt with the way Marie Antoinette had in mind. The owner of the nest has to say, and I paraphrase.

"There's no free bread here, go eat cake." And fortunately that is my last foray into politics, back to the brats of Marginal Waters.

What are we a box of gerbils?

Two long time brats of Marginal Waters sat on a picnic table near the end of the dock. Usually they had no problems talking but today, well to day was different, way different. Different on the bad side for a kid is when your old life just blows up, leaving nothing behind but uncertainty. It has been my observation that children do not prosper under uncertainty. And though this particular story is a little unusual, families falling apart is a very usual story.

The kids in question had been boating buddies for years under significantly better circumstances. The boy in the twosome remained a little bit confused by recent events.

"So what exactly is going on?" The girl seemed to have a better grasp of this unfolding story.

"Well my mom and your dad are going to buy a new boat and house, and my dad and your mom are going to buy a new boat and house." He asked just to make sure,

"Together!" She rolled her eyes.

"Yeah together." He thought for a minute.

"So…." Emma delivered the obvious news.

"Yep, I'm 'fraid so." Danny nodded, he got it but just had to make sure.

“So they’re switching.” Emma nodded.

“Yep.” Danny had a good question.

“Why?” She patted him on the back.

“Haven’t a clue, let me know if you figure it out.”

I digress briefly again into amateur psychology; I always assumed that marriages break up and half of them do over either resentment or boredom. Question is which is the most common? Or is my definition too simplistic? I look forward to hearing your theories around the campfire as my own understanding of human behaviour is sketchy to say the least, and I seem to have less rather than more insight the older I get. I know when it comes to kids the reasons are irrelevant, for them it just stinks. Danny asked.

“So are we going to be step brother and step sister now?” Emma who was not any happier about this than Danny tried to make light of it.

“I guess, so I suppose we can’t have sex any more.” That at least gave Danny a laugh and gave her a little punch on the shoulder.

“That’s kind of funny.” They both sat thinking about the latest turn of events to seriously complicate both their families. Finally Danny came up with a logistical question.

“So where are we supposed to go?” He at least had figured out that he was going to leave, or maybe not, but to where or where not was the question.

“Well Bud I think we’re supposed to figure out who we’re going to live with. You want a new mom or a new dad?” Danny now got angry.

“I don’t want either!” She added

“I don’t think they care what we think.” He added.

“And what about our old boats and houses?” Emma shrugged.

“Sold I guess.” Danny still didn’t get it.

“Why don’t they just move boats?”

“My mom says too many memories.” The poor lad just shook his head and they both sat, trying to make sense of all this.

“So I guess we can still hang out.” His long time friend was now starting to get upset.

“Oh yeah, for now and pretend everything is fine; it also depends where they buy the new houses? We might have to go to new schools; you want that?” The answer of course was obvious for Danny.

"No!" He thought for a minute. "The hell with them all, I think we should run away." That was not even close to what she thought he would say.

"Us, where, how?"

"Canoe, cross the lake, down the river, camping, fishing, for the summer, long as we can; a kid's water trip." She tried to make a joke out of his idea

"Like Bonnie and Clyde without the sex and bank robbing." Danny gave her a little nudge.

"There you go." Emma pointed out the obvious.

"They'd just send the cops after us." Her long time buddy grinned.

"They got to find us first; think about it, maybe they won't even bother, too busy, you know." That brought out a blush.

"I don't even want to think about that." Danny had another thought.

"Why didn't they just buy a big boat and one big house and we could all live together like a box of gerbils?" Emma hit him.

"Don't suggest that might even get them thinking." Danny scoffed.

“I think there’s just one thing on their minds.” She blushed again at the thought.

“Let’s not think about that.” Not an unusual reaction, it seems that every generation thinks it invented sex and all past generations who did it and still do it are disgusting.

Plank Number One: Clue Number Two

Emma burst out of her little cabin into the main salon.

"Ta da!" There she stood all scrubbed, fluffed, polished, and smiling; her parents looked up from their morning coffee somewhat surprised. Her dad looked at Emma and asked,

"Who is this again?" She stuck her tongue at at him.

"It's your smart and charming daughter." This was new as questions were usually answered in monosyllabic grunts and nods as her personality slowly ran up through the gears reaching operational capacity around lunchtime. Actually most teenagers aren't much good in the morning; I'm sure many of you have tried to get them out of bed for school and if you think that's hard try teaching them something at nine in the morning. Her mom was amazed.

"Em what's going on, and what are you wearing?" It was the shirt Jack and Charlie had given her. She spun around and held out her arms so they could see the caption on the back. Her dad asked hoping it wasn't some kind of cult, although in some ways it is.

"What is the Order of the Woodpecker?" Emma shrugged.

“People who like and work on wooden boats.” Her dad was incredulous.

“You are going to work on a wooden boat, in the morning!” Emma shrugged and grabbed an orange off the table.

“Yep, summer project; keep me off the pole.” If you hadn’t figured it out yet Emma was smart, really good at thinking on her feet and quite often she liked to mess with people especially her parents’ to amuse herself. Her mom smiled noticing a definite increase in Emma’s morning fluffing. Her pony tail hairdo was a little higher and fluffier and there was the pleasant subtle scent of Emma’s favourite perfume drifted through the salon on their boat. Her mom smiled and asked.

“And might there be a boy involved?” Emma was not interested in giving a lot of details.

“Hints and allegations, I’ll be down at the work slip near the shop at the end of the marina.” Both of her parents were silently very happy, even if there was a boy in the picture this would be a daylight rendezvous, Emma had a definite bounce in her step; if you’re going to have a teenager around, best to have a happy one with something to do they like. Her mom had to ask.

"And does the boy have a name?" Emma came over and sat down constructing a story on the way. She put her elbows on the table and chin on folded hands, figuring she'd have some fun.

"Well his name is Doobie, you know, cause he…" She held a pretend marihuana cigarette in her hand and pretended to take a puff. " And he's in a band, drummer, just plays with his left hand now, cause." Her parents had caught on many words ago but let her daughter play this one out. "He's got carpal tunnel in his right shoulder, too much masturbating." Her dad held up his hand to hopefully stop her talking.

"Yeah, get out of here, rotten smart ass kid." Emma gave them her best evil grin and bounded for the door. Her mother called after her.

"Glad you happy sweetheart." With that the occasionally but currently not truculent daughter bounced down the dock, singing.

"I love rock and roll, so put another dime in the jukebox baby." Her parents turned to each other and clicked coffee mugs; their wackadoodle daughter was happy and life was looking pretty good. They both had the summer off and were looking forward to it. Then daughter reappeared sticking her head around the door frame. She grinned.

“You got rid of me, now you can have nautical morning sex after breakfast.” Her dad called out.

“That’s it….” and bolted after her but she just giggled and ran down the dock, much faster than her old dad. He came back and sat down smiling,

“Not a bad idea.”

Emma bounced down the dock, feeling good, she was a little excited about being able to delve into a mystery, and mother nature was working on her as she does. She liked Sam, but for no specific reason she could think of. She thought, once he gets his eyes off Mary’s butt he was pretty good company and she had to admit, not bad looking. With her thinking over she arrived Baby Bootlegger’s dock.

“Morning Mr. Woodpecker.” Sam looked up and smiled.

“Morning yourself, Miss Woodpecker,” he patted the plank set up along side the boat, “take a seat. I made the staging a little wider so you don’t fall in the water.”

“Not because my butt’s big.” Sam blushed,

“No and your butt’s not big.” She moved a little closer, deciding messing with him was fun.

“So you checked it out already?” He figured he’d dodge the obvious answer to that question and picked up his X-acto knife.

“Your butt’s fine, let’s get to work.” She sat there for a second then decided not to let him off the hook yet.

“How fine, it’s behind me so, I don’t see it.” She smiled at him again, waiting for an answer. He decided to ignore her, not having a witty reply and truthfully, some questions are best left unanswered.

“I’ll work at the other end of the plank.” They sat and pried out bungs, amazingly losing track of time, both finding it surprisingly relaxing and they felt productive. As a work spot it wasn’t bad as the boat was under cover so they were in the shade and it was a pleasantly warm summer morning. After about an hour Mary appeared out of nowhere.

“Hey Sammy, hey Emma, he been nice?” Emma smiled,

“Not bad actually, you know, for a boy.” Sam protested.

“Hey!” Mary just laughed and sat down a small cooler.

“There’s cold water in there; we’ll bring you lunch later.” Emma was surprised.

“Really.” Mary headed back up the stairs and Sam couldn’t resist one quick look at her butt.

“Yep you’re a woodpecker, got to feed the woodpeckers.” Then called out, “Sammy stop staring at my butt.” Sam turned to Emma.

“How does she know?” Emma rolled her eyes.

“We’re not stupid you know.” Sam at that point figured he’d stay out of trouble by getting back to work. They continued working until they had the plank almost loose both arriving at the last set of bungs and screws. They were sitting close enough to touch, just a little self conscious, not really knowing what to think about any of this. Emma giggled.

“Look at us, side by side; you don’t smell bad for a boy.” Sam sniffed.

“You smell really nice, you wear perfume?” She blushed a little, but always with a smart remark.

“No it’s my natural aura.” Sam’s forehead wrinkled, again couldn’t think of anything clever to say. She gave him the application details.

“I spray it in the air and run through it.”

“Why?” She thought about that as she got ready to pull the last screw.

“I don’t know really, I’m a girl so I guess so I smell nice, my mom taught me how to do it. She says a woman doesn’t have to be overpowering just alluring.” Sam just sat thinking about what she said and had no reply mainly because he wasn’t sure what alluring meant but it sounded good, He finally came up with,

“Cool, ok, ready, the plank should come out.” Sure enough it almost fell in their laps. Then Mary appeared again with another cooler and singer Emma. Girl Emma looked up and studied woman Emma for a minute, she pieced it together.

“You’re, you’re Emily Larson! What are you doing here?” She just smiled having had that reception in the past but now she was commonly accepted as one of the inmates.

“I live here; sort of hiding out for ....I don’t know.” Sam informed her.

“She sings for us around the fire sometimes, it’s really nice.” Emma was more than impressed.

"I like this place even more." Emily noticed what seemed to be a very new couple and just smiled thinking, must be the air in this place. She turned and left,

"Enjoy your lunch." As Emma munched on her sandwich she mumbled.

"She is so so beautiful." Sam picked up his water bottle and held it up and looked at Emma.

"There's lots of beautiful girls around here." She blushed a little, surprised but of course pleased.

"Me?" Sam said, surprising himself by his smoothness.

"Of course you, you're the only girl around now." They left it at that and sat on the dock eating their lunch both thinking, this is nice, but being young weren't completely sure why yet. But as stated in other books they were discovering an important way to a happy life. Find something you like to do and someone to care about. And I don't think it matters, a good friend, light romance, a serious romance or children, important parts of all lives.

With lunch done they looked inside what was now a long gap in Baby Bootlegger. They were both excited, realizing there were more clues to the mystery yet to be found. Emma stuck her head inside and spotted something, and reached up near the inside of the deck.

"Look what I found." She came out and inside a zip lock bag was what looked like a new cell phone. She took it out. "What's this about?" Sam said,

"See if it powers up." They sat together as the phone powered up and soon what they saw was even more amazing. It was a older man's face.

"That's my Pops, dead now." Emma stared.

"Wow, well not there." Good old Pops had been electronically resurrected; it was a pre-recorded video, all cued up. Emma pressed the run arrow and it started. The face started talking.

"Well hello again Sam. if you're watching this I'm guessing you're all in. So you need more information, you will likely receive some visitors over the next few days. You should talk to them." The kids just looked at each other having no idea where this was going but knew they were on the cusp of a collection of stories, and don't we all love stories.

"You should know I have money, well had, don't have anything right now, actually there's a little over ten million dollars, and I can't spend it so after you talk to the people who come to see you, you decide how much to give them." The kids eyes just kept getting wider. "I decided trust you rather than some lawyer to make the call. When you decide, give my lawyer a call, you met him and he will transfer the money. Don't want you responsible for that He paused for a minute. "Or of course you can ask him to transfer it all out to yourself or anywhere you want." He gave a little smile into the camera. "Nothing I can do about it, but, somehow I don't think you'll do that. I chose you by the way because I trust you to be honourable and I think you're a better man as a boy than I was as a man.

The people who may come are the ones you found in the book; I'm sure you've found it, if not, start looking. They are women I've known in my past and have not treated very well. It was suggested I make amends, so I'm going to try, with your help. You can do what you want but in my opinion, keep the adult supervision on this to a minimum. I've found many of them rather devious and unreliable, especially myself. Well that's about it, I've said my piece and I leave it all up to you. Oh and one last thing, please, please, find someone to care about and look after them." His voice choked for the first time. "I never did."

The video turned off and a bank web site appeared showing the exact amount in the account.

$10,381,427.16

Emma came to first and quoted one of the many lines she got from being taken to Shakespearian plays by her family.

"The game is afoot!" Sam just looked at her, agreeing in his own way.

"Wow, wow, this is way out big, big huge! What the heck am I supposed to do with all this?" Sam was more than a little overwhelmed. "I don't even know where to start, maybe I should tell my parents." Emma knew that was probably a good idea but this was the most exciting thing that had happened to her in her young life and wasn't initially keen on sharing her adventure with anybody, especially her parents. She pointed out.

"So someone, a woman is going to drop by soon; what's the harm in talking to them, get their story?" Sam had been thinking and came to the same conclusion and asked.

“Can’t see any harm in that; you want to help?” Emma was excited.

“Of course I do; thanks for asking.” Sam was feeling much better, not really looking forward to doing all this on his own mainly because he had no idea where to start; I think most of us wouldn’t.

“What do you think I should ask?” Emma had been thinking about that; she thought about a lot of things.

“Well the one really important question is how did they know Pops.” Sam nodded.

“Ok, guess we just wait, want a swimming lesson?” Emma gave him a poke with her finger.

“You just want to see me in a bathing suit.” That of course had crossed his mind. He blushed and asked.

“Is it a bikini?” She just smiled a little flirtatiously.

“Not telling.”

Danny and Emma's Voyage to ?

For the second set of brats in the marina things weren't going quite as well. Most children don't make plans to run away from their parents, unless there are unusual circumstances but still this was a huge step for anyone, never mind fairly young kids. For many kids when it comes to running it does not usually go well whether they stay lost or whether they are returned to their parents. Danny and Emma had talked and figured they probably wouldn't get very far but maybe at least they could make a point.

The preliminary plans had been made under the not so watchful eye of either set of parents, both whose lives were occupied with other issues. Equipment and other supplies were gathered and stored then the plan was under the cover of almost morning darkness the two kids with full camping gear loaded their canoe would head out onto the lake. The plan was to get off the lake and into the river, hopefully before anyone knew they were gone. Then the question would be which river; they knew someone would be looking for them, probably pretty fast.

A good idea, absolutely not, at thirteen, way too young to be on your own with no real destination or plan in mind.

They had discussed how this might affect their parents but Danny had an opinion.

"I care as much as they do."

So early one morning after all the planning was done the intrepid travellers set sail, i.e. paddle across the flat water of Lake Couchiching, heading north into a maze of rivers and lakes, full of back channels and blind bays. The final destination was not known, just not here. They both had spent a lot of time around water and on boats and had done a fair amount of camping so were familiar with being on the water. They had packed staples for the trip, the rest would be filled in with fish, wild blueberries and raspberries. Also figuring they could mooch the occasional meal from other campers and boaters. They had a bit of money with them just in case, but it wouldn't go far.

The evening of day one had been successful, tents pitched, camp set, full tummies, fresh pickerel cooked on a primus stove, no campfire to draw attention, and in a back channel with no cottages. Lots of places to hide in northern Ontario if you don't want to be found. Once the sun had gone down it was safe to light a fire. They had also camped on a small island, much safer as fewer creatures will venture into black water on a whim.

They sat looking up at the stars sipping hot chocolate.

"Not bad eh Danny?" Danny nodded.

"Not bad at all. I bet all hell's been breaking out all day at headquarters." Emma was not concerned, as far as she was concerned they were all bought and paid for.

"To hell with them." Then being a girl got a little emotional and practical at the same time. "Where are we going?" Danny was more angry and less thoughtful about all this.

"Well, west and sort of north. I remember a movie I saw, a couple were going to run away and the girl said.

I'd like to go west in a car I can't afford with a plan I don't have." That got a little laugh out of Emma, then she said.

"We got the no plan part, and here's another topic for discussion, are we a couple?" This was a completely new topic for Danny. He looked over at the face he'd seen a thousand times and answered truthfully.

"I don't know." He didn't say any more and there was a long pause then surprised the heck out of Emma and said. "I don't know about you be I don't want anything to mess things up. You're my best friend and I want it to stay that way." Danny interrupted.

"Like our families." He thought for a moment. "You know we're all that's left of both our families." Danny lifted his cup of hot chocolate and they clicked.

"Well, here's to sticking together." Emma reached out and took his hand. It was actually the first time she'd ever touched him or he her, other than the occasional push and pretend shoulder punch when she beat him at poker or something.

They sat is the gathering darkness of a warm summer evening and stared at the campfire; it had the same soothing effect it must have had on millions of camper, hunters gathers and explorers down through the ages. It provided some safety from wild animals, warmth and the source of a warm dinner. Both were wondering what happens tomorrow, and the day after that, and so on. They would soon be tired enough to sleep and for few hours and for a while everything would be fine.

Release the Dogs of War II

Leah and Eddy sat on the end of the dock, the spot usually reserved for Skid Row Geezers, Charlie and Jack, the Happy Gang and any other adults that wanted to gather. Kids occasionally came down to swim under adult supervision of course. This morning the dock was deserted, to early for the geezers most of whom would be asleep, or some would be off looking for someone that might be brewing free coffee. Jack and Charlie were off moving a boat and the Happy Gang were hard at work. Leah had an idea.

"You know how the adults are always organizing Beer Pong battles, Rendezvous and other stuff. Eddy nodded.

"Yep, just an excuse to drink beer." Once again the high ground so easily attainable when you're on your own and with no parents or other adults to overhear, and perhaps they're right. Leah said,

"We should organize a…mosh up, kids only." Eddy laughed,

"A mosh up, what's that?"

"A party, gig, a happening." Eddy agreed.

"Good idea, remember Release the Dogs of War?" Leah laughed as well.

“That was fun to watch, we could have one of our own.” Leah added.

“Not the same, that would be copying.” They knew they needed something on their own, kids only of course, but different. The question was what? How do you fashion a little high jinx without getting too far outside the box and have your parents throwing fit or getting grounded for a month? They sat for a bit pondering, like their parents and other members of Marginal Waters, just staring out at the lake.

I’ve spent many an hour with whiskey in hand just staring out at the water from my fine vantage point at Marginal Waters. Why do we do that by the way? Here I go again, my own theory is we realize that water is our primordial ooze, our very distant ancestors crawled out of some shallow pond, and we are perhaps drawn to our genetic beginning, or the explorers in us see it as a natural highway to adventure, well who knows really, ask around, or come up with your own, I like theories.

Back to Leah and Eddy’s dilemma, how to push the envelope of fun and extend the leash without getting grounded for the balance of the summer.

Leah had an idea.

“How about organize a naval battle?” Eddy’s brain was headed the wrong way.

“How do you fight with belly buttons?” Leah laughed and pushed her brother over.”

“Really, Eddy, you’ve had too many pucks to the melon? No some kind of nerf war on water, kids only.”

“How we going to do that, we need boats.” They both sat there thinking and came up with the same name at the same time.

“Tommy.” Wisely choosing the grass to run on they blasted towards where Tom usually hung out in the morning. Sure enough there he was opening up the gas docks. Eddy got out of the way down.

“You do the talking.” They panted to a stop.

“Tommy.” He heard them coming and looked up.

“Hello darlin’, Eddy.” Eddy smiled to himself thinking always send a girl to do the talking to another guy, even the little ones seemed to have a touch. Leah had rehearsed as much of the proposal as she had.

“Tommy we want to organize a kid’s water war, but we need boats.” Tom nodded.

"Sounds fun, ok, can't use dinghies though, they have motors and might get damaged." Leah gave him the pout. Tom was thinking.

"Make some boats out of cardboard and duct tape." Eddy liked the idea of that.

"How we do that?" Tom pointed, he had an idea and also this deflect the question to someone else, and he had work to do.

"I know Robert the Mutant built them as a kid, go talk to him." They were off like a flash arriving at Robert's boat. He was varnishing as usual with Christian Island playing in the background. They knew better than to bother him until he finished the panel he was working on, so they stood back arms folded waiting semi-patiently. He finally looked up.

"Monsters." He always called them that though he really liked them; they had energy; he appreciated energy in a place that in his opinion seemed to have a permanent energy crisis. Leah again,

"Robert you know how to build a boat out of cardboard and duct tape?" He smiled remembering his youth on Hamilton Bay and Lake Ontario. Completely unsupervised as a young teen he and his buddies built many cardboard boats, playing naval battles with water balloons until their 'ships' sank. On light wind days they would paddle out into Lake Ontario on inner tubes till you could just see the shore. Not a good idea by the way for any young readers. Robert came back to the present.

"Of course I do, find some cardboard and duct tape." Off like a flash heading back towards Tommy who saw them coming and didn't have time to hide. They arrived, he noted hardly out of breath.

"Tommy we need cardboard and duct tape." Just then Tess came out of the office and was instantly curious.

"What's going on?" The kids told Tess about what they had in mind. Well soon thanks to Charlie and singer Emma piles of new cardboard and a couple of cases of duct tape where found. Teams were formed and the kids went off into their various corners to construct their warships. The Dogs of War were to be released again at Marginal Waters but before anyone could too far into it Tess came around and posted the rules of engagement on many of the poles around the marina. She called it…

Trafalgar 'ish'

1. All sailors must wear life jackets.

2. The only weapons allowed are Marginal Waters standard issue lances: a 12" nerf ball mounted on eight foot bamboo pole.

3. The lance may not be swung, only used like a lance not like a baseball bat.

4. All boats are made of cardboard and duct tape only. Maximum of three crew per boat, powered by paddles only.

5. You are out of the battle if your boat sinks or all your crew members are in the water, or show any signs of excessive violence, or more seriously give the 'Admiral' any back talk.

6. The Admiral of the Fleet is Tess Lannigan. I will oversee the battle and call your boat or crew out. Any violation of the above rules; you are out, my decisions are final. Don't mess with a girl that hasn't bought a new pair of shoes in three months.

7. Remember we are here to have fun, get wet and then have a party.

8. P.S. Spectators are required to contribute ten dollars to the Marginal Waters party fund (not kidding), goes to buy nerf balls and beer, and the Tess Lannigan shoe fund. (kidding)

9. All party goers that eat are required to bring something to the pot luck. Skid Row geezers take a special note!

10. Final note, anyone spraying water on the Admiral will be keel hauled!

Mary and her Mother

Emma and Sam sat looking at today's project, plank number two, number one sure was interesting, not so much the plank but what they found under it. They were both slow to start working both wondering and waiting on who their first visitor might be. Emma finally said,

"Well what do you think?" Sam picked up his X-acto knife.

"That plank ain't going to take itself off." Then Emma noticed first and whispered.

"Your girlfriend is coming down the dock." Sam looked up and rolled his eyes; it was getting a little old.

"She's not my girlfriend." Emma just smiled and put her hands up.

"Ok, whatever you say." Mary stopped where they were sitting, then sat down next to Sam. He thought, this is new, and the old crush came to the surface, but he was determined to be cool. Truthfully, in a moment of personal growth, not wanting to offend Emma. He asked.

"What's up Mary?" She seemed nervous.

"My mom's freaking out." This was a shock for Mary who for years had been the one freaking out and her mother was the rock, now something was definitely up. Emma figured she'd stay out of this, watching with interest the interaction between Sam and Mary.

"She got a call last night, she's been drinking wine ever since." Emma gave Sam a look and Mary noticed. "You know something about this?" Sam asked but already knew.

"Who was it from?"

"The old guy, who died? Can a ghost use a phone?" Sam just said,

"Pops is at the bottom of this, your mom needs to come down and talk to me." Mary didn't get it.

"About what?" Sam just shrugged.

"I can't say, but who was the call for?"

"For mom." That settled it for Sam

"She should to talk to me, I know sounds weird, but trust me, she should." Mary jumped up, looking for an early solution to help and hopefully cure her newly neurotic mother from slipping into alcoholism like her good old departed dad.

"Ok, I'll go and get her, might stop her drinking." She disappeared down the dock leaving the kids. Emma added.

"This could get a little complicated; maybe we should tell our parents." Sam was not in such a hurry now and wanted to try this one his own, and truthfully nothing bad had happened so far.

"Not yet." Soon Mary re-appeared with her mother in tow; she did not look too happy and Sam was feeling more and more uncomfortable about this, temporarily rethinking his idea not to involve his parents. Absolutely not a situation most kids would find themselves in. I think most adult readers would want their kids to talk to them?

They all sat down at the picnic table in front of Baby Bootlegger. Mary's mom kept looking at the boat and at Sam and Emma. Emma caught on real early, there was some kind of major unpublished back story. Finally Sam said.

"Mrs. Hinson, this is Emma," he paused trying to figure out exactly how to describe her. "She's a friend and going to sit with us if you don't mind. She's helping me out with all this." Mary's mom was wondering what all this was, what she had so far was anything but good.

Mary's mom had a raft of feelings that had been brought back to the surface. Uncomfortable would not even be close to how she felt at the moment, surrounded by kids who she figured would not understand, especially one in particular. But she just nodded, in some ways intrigued by the mystery of being contacted by a man that was dead and although she had an idea where part of this was going, the rest was a bit of a mystery. This was obviously planned before he died, why would be a good question. Finally she just nodded; and Sam being a boy and also being coached by quite smart Emma got to the point.

“Mrs. Hinson, how did you know Pops?” She bowed her head and thought, yes sir, hit the nail right on the button, and that was the big question; amazing how she got right to it. She looked up and then at both kids and her daughter, wishing she had brought the wine bottle with her. But she did have a question.

“Sam why do I need to talk about this anyway.” Sam in a moment of advanced cool in his opinion said,

“Pops left his business with me, don’t know why but it is what it is.” Emma had a good thought and said,

“Truly it’s up to you; but you really should to talk to us and I can leave if you want but you should know either way anything said at this table, stays here.” Sam nodded in agreement; he hadn’t thought about saying that but it sure seemed like a good idea. He and Emma had also talked about the money and Emma suggested with people, keep the promise of money out of it until you got what appeared to be the truth because as we know, people will often lie when it improves their relative position, especially financially.

Mrs. Hinson decided to tell the truth that maybe should have been told years ago. She took a deep breath and thought, here goes.

"Pops and I go a way back." She looked at Mary. "Your dad was off on one of his find his walkabouts. That usually involved other women and lots of beer. She looked at her daughter. "You know him as well as me." Mary just nodded, that part was certainly true. "I was alone, again, feeling sorry for myself. I remember sitting on the back of my boat when Pops wandered by. She remembered the exact words.

"Darly why so glum?" I just shrugged and he said, "Want a boat ride, blow the cobwebs out of your brain, got a fresh bottle of fifteen year old scotch, we can sit out on the lake and get drunk, watch the sun go down, the hell with everything and everybody." He had a knack of appearing around the marina at the right time, and at the time it sounded better than being alone." Mary interjected.

"With Pops, he's old." Her mother smiled.

"This was a few years ago, so then not so much, and with Pops, part of his charm was he never promised anything, just a boat ride on a summer night and good scotch, that's all. You saw what you got and though that was not much, all cards such as they were, were on the table." Mary said,

"So..." Her mother nodded

"Fraid so," she paused not sure how her daughter would react.

"Long story short, that night...he's your dad, or was." She closed her eyes afraid of the look that might be on her daughter's face. When she opened them Mary was gone, heading down the dock at a good clip. Her mother got up to go after he but Emma suggested, remembering how her dad treated her when she had one of her mini meltdowns.

"Let her walk it off, cool down." Mary stopped at the end of the dock and looked at the water for the longest time. She went into her boat and came back with a few glasses and a bottle of wine. She sat down.

"Who's drinking other than me?" Sam just shook his head; Emma said,

"I'd be grounded for the rest of the summer." Mary's mom just nodded and Mary filled both glasses and took a sip.

Mary's mom figured when she came back she would need something from the bar. She put the bottle down and sat down next to her mother. She looked at the wine and her mother just nodded, so she took a sip.

"Mom, I never really knew who I thought was my dad, he was never around, and Pops, never knew him at all. Neither one cared about me at all, you did, always have." She put her arm around her and kissed her on the cheek. "Always will."

Sam and Emma were more than pleased, finally Sam let out a deep breath,

"So you guys are good?" Mary kissed her mom again and said,

"We're good." Mary's mom's eyes were full of tears, happy ones. She wrapped her arms around her daughter and gave her a long affectionate hug. Sam got to the other side of the story.

"What do you guys need, money wise?" Mary seldom missing anything asked,

"Why?" Sam said,

"Pops left money, he had a plan to makes things sort of right after his death, so what do you need, he's paying? Mary and her mother looked at each other. Finally Mary's mother spoke.

"I have a good job, house, boat." She put her arm around her daughter again. "And my girl here, I'm good, really, Pops doesn't owe me anything." Mary said,

"I got a job I like and good friends." She leaned her head on her mother's shoulder, nothing else was needed. Then she sat up.

"Do we have to spend the money on ourselves?" Sam and Emma looked at each other thinking. Emma just gave Sam a look. Sam said,

"That's your call." Mary looked at her mom.

"Mom let's go for a walk, I got a plan."

Misguided Angel?

From the outset Jenny was what you would call an unusual girl even as a very young child, often prone to daydreaming, wandering off to sit by herself and stare out at the water, up at the sky, or studying a little bug, lost in her own thoughts. Some might say even as a child fitting right in with the collection of unusual characters at Marginal Waters. Her distracted behaviour was a constant topic of conversation at parent teacher interviews from the time Jenny was in kindergarten. The comment often went like this.

"If Jenny would just apply herself a little harder." But Jenny was just fine, a happy confident charming child and growing up at her own pace.

As she got older and the natural leash got longer she was allowed alone daydream down time, as her parents put it, realizing their little girl needed this. It was basically harmless and it just was the way she was.

Jenny by the time she was twelve had come up with her favourite form of daydream, the night dream. She was naturally drawn to the water as the sun went down and wind dropped. On warm summer nights she would paddled out into the shallow swamp behind the marina and just float around.

lying down in her canoe with her head on a pillow and look for shooting stars, running the count up in her head until her dad came down to the dock and called her in.

She was on her one of her new moon paddles through the swamp as she called them. Her parents were never very pleased about this because it was absolutely pitch black but reluctantly allowed her to go because she would always sit out at the end of the dock looking sad until her parents relented and let her go. Her dad was always concerned.

"What if a boat runs into you, you've got no lights?" She would just shrug.

"Dad no power boats go in the swamp, too shallow I could get out and walk if I needed to, it's all good."

When she got to sixteen and it was really warm and windless she would take a sleeping bag with her and sleep in her canoe all night, her canoe held loosely by a small anchor. Her mom always concerned as well.

"Jenny aren't you afraid out there all alone?" Jenny was not, after a day a week at school, surrounded by babbling teachers 'applying herself' as required and chattering classmates she looked forward to night of looking at the stars, and listening to music on her phone. Her dad who actually was similar used to say.

"Jenny, you're just like the family cat, comfortable with your own resources." But he was still concerned even though she would always remind her parents that she was about ten minutes from home and she had a phone.

On one particular night she noticed out on the swamp she was not alone, a dim light was glowing over the black water where no lights should be. She was initially annoyed wondering if someone else had moved into her Saturday hide out. Curious about it she started paddling towards the light. She could see it wasn't a flashlight or boat's running light just the dimmest glowing object; it seemed to be floating just above the water. She initially thought it might be a Chinese Lantern but it didn't move.

As she got closer she could see the light was coming from inside a boat that was drifting in the middle of the swamp like her. Out of the black night appeared the silhouette of a long narrow runabout illuminated only by starlight and a dim glow coming form inside the boat. She was starting to get a little spooked by this as there appeared to be nobody on board; she wondered maybe it had drifted away from a dock or worse somebody had fallen overboard and drowned just like her parents were always worried she might do.

When she got right up to the boat she could see it was Baby Bootlegger a boat and owner from the marina that she knew well. She spoke out loud.

"I know this boat." Then she heard a loud booming and drunken voice come out of the boat.

"Get the fuck out of here!" Jenny had just reached the side of the boat and put her hands on the gunnels and looked inside. There he was, Pops in one of his familiar poses, falling down drunk was lying flat on his back across the boat's seat with a whiskey bottle in his hands, the engine hatches were up, that's where the light was coming from. Pops looked up in a complete alcoholic haze and saw Jenny looking down at him and tried to struggle to sit up.

"I said get...." He had been drinking whiskey all evening, straight from the bottle, hoping to pass out before the booze ran out. All he got out was part of the sentence as he passed out dropping his whiskey bottle in the bilge. In the quiet of the night Jenny could hear the whiskey gurgling out of the narrow opening in the bottle then there was a flash of blue flame. The whiskey had run towards what was later determined a candle burning in a metal tray screwed to a wood frame under the boat's engine, some vaporized and ignited, turning Baby Bootlegger into a wooden flambé. Fire on any powerboat is most serious mainly because most of them hold many gallons of gasoline.

Fortunately Jenny was in a lot better shape than Pops and grabbed the portable fire extinguisher in the runabout's helm and emptied it into Baby Bootlegger's bilge. She leaned on the gunnels breathing hard, but the fire was out. Pops didn't look too good but he appeared to be alive. With hands shaking she found her phone.

"Dad, I'm ok, get Tommy to come out to the swamp, Baby Bootlegger's floating and Pops is passed out; yeah I'm ok. Can you come too?"

Jenny sat down in her canoe shaking, thinking, I could use some of that whiskey the got burned up. Tom arrived with Jenny's dad and Bill with the Coast Guard boat.

"What's going on Jen?" She told him the story while Bill and his crew started working on Pops. Bill looked down at the passed out old goat, thinking, where have I seen that before.

“Been drinking on the water again you old fart.” One of his men grumbled.

“Let’s just shoot him.” Bill nodded in agreement, he had no sense of humour about drunken boaters, seen the down side of this activity too many times.

Tom in the meantime was prowling around Baby Bootlegger making sure there was no chance it would catch on fire again and found the candle. He came up out of the engine hatch.

“The candle was under a fuel line, Pops was trying to kill himself, the old Viking funeral.” Jenny’s dad put her arm around her.

“You could have been killed.” Well Baby Bootlegger got towed back to the marina and old Pops was hauled away to hospital to have his stomach pumped and get re-hydrated. Some might ask, why do we bother with people like that?

The next day the angel herself went to visit him, for some reason still concerned for the old drunk. She found him looking a little better dozing in his hospital bed. She stood over him for a minute then whispered,

"Pops." His eyes opened and recognized Jenny and knowing immediately he had been saved and was not thankful.

"What you do that for?"

"Your boat was going to blow up!" He turned away.

"That's what I wanted." Bits and pieces were starting to come back to him. He turned away snarling.

"You should have let me die." Jenny just stared at him.

"Why?" He looked back, wondering why she was spending any time with him at all, in his view a completely lost cause.

"I've done nothing but wrong everywhere all of my life, I've had enough." She sat pulled up a chair and sat down beside his bed.

"But I gave you time." He was still not impressed with his gift and I suppose when you decide to commit suicide you don't want any more time. He could see no use for it.

"Time for what?" She thought for a minute.

"Well maybe time for you to make amends." Jenny had been around the marina long enough to know something about Pops; the stories she heard were not good. He was not initially interested in making amends, turning away from her again.

"It's too late for that." Jenny pulled her chair closer.

"I know some of the things you've done, they can all be fixed, not completely but pretty close. Her blue eyes seemed to be getting bluer, and Pops was really starting to wonder about this girl, but could still see no point to any of this.

"Girl all my stories are bad." Jenny would not let it go.

"Pops, there's only one story, good and evil, right and wrong, do what's good and right, make amends." Old Pop's actually pulled himself up in bed.

"What are you some kind of angel?" Jenny just smiled and gave him a little pat on the shoulder.

"Well maybe I am, let's go with that." He was still not convinced.

"Well if you are you're misguided." She leaned over and patted him on the arm again.

"No I'm not, make amends, fix the things that are fixable; you'll feel better." Then she said sternly, "Give you something to do besides drink." With that she turned and left, she'd said her piece. He called out.

"Will you come to see me again." Without turning back she just said,

"No." Thinking at the same time, I've said my piece and I've had enough of you.

Not long after that Pops really did die, not with a planned Viking funeral but a major artery blew out in his sleep. His body was not in the best of shape, years of heavy drinking, bad diet and cigar smoking had taken its toll. But as you know on the bright side he took the angel's advice and perhaps knowing he was running out of time at least tried to make amends.

Never Invite a Raccoon Into Your Nest, Even a Charming One

Baby Bootlegger sat with two long rectangular holes in its side, the planks had covered up a lot more than just long holes in the side of the boat as the kids found they both had stories under them. Miss and young Mister Woodpecker were on their usual morning perch waiting to tackle plank three, wondering what was under it when a rusty three quarter length school bus pulled up and squeaked to a stop right behind their work slip. Both kids knew immediately that something was up. Soon a middle aged woman got out and walked right over towards the two kids. She asked looking right at Sam,

"Are you Sam Clarkson?" Sam nodded, both kids watching as one after another, kids from ten to maybe eighteen started getting off the bus. They all just stood quietly next to it, saying nothing. Finally Emma came to and asked.

"Can we help you?" The woman sighed; she looked tired.

"Came a long way, so I hope so." Emma asked pointing to the kids.

"Are they all yours?" The woman smiled.

“Well yes, sort of.” Sam and Emma wondered, what the heck? This had to be something to do with Pops, could good old Pops have fathered what looked to be a soccer team with subs. Sam said politely.

“Have a seat miss,” and fished out a bottle of water for her. Both kids were wondering as we all would, what kind of story goes with a woman and a bus load of kids that are not biologically hers. The woman could see their faces were full of questions.

“I’m Darlene Mitchell, these are my kids, not mine by birth, more of a collection of.” She was searching the right words, “ Like stray kittens. I got a call from Pops, that’s why I’m here.”

Emma had an idea.

“I’m going to talk to Mary and Emma, get these kids some washrooms and something to eat.” Darlene was very thankful,

“Thank you, been a long drive.” Emma waved at the crowd waiting patiently.

“Come on guys, let’s get some food.” As she headed up to the loft of the Happy Gang’s workshop she looked back and sure enough they were all following her obediently.

Well soon washrooms were found and all kids were sitting on the Happy Gang's overhead deck munching on one of singer Emily's now famous BLT sandwiches. People were looked after; such was life at Marginal Waters. Emma had returned to the picnic table, not wanting to miss out of anything. Darlene turned to Emma.

"Thanks again for looking after them, let me tell my story." Sam just sat there, not even venturing an idea as to where does a woman come up with seventeen kids, none of them hers, and what was Pops' connection?

"I got a call, that's why I'm here, haven't seen Pops in maybe five years, how is he?" Sam gave her the news.

"He died, just recently; the call was pre-recorded, about making amends." Emma studied the woman's face looking for some remorse at hearing that Pops had died, if there was it was subtle.

"I got that from the call; I guess he knew he was on the way out." Emma added.

"He actually tried to kill himself a few months ago." Just then Emily the singer came down from the deck with a sandwich and a big glass of wine. She sat it down.

“I’m guessing you could use lunch yourself and something from the bar.” She smiled and looked up.

“Thank you…hey you’re, the cook, you’re Emily Larson!” Emily smiled back.

“Yes, this is my hide out.” She held one finger to her lips. “Shhh.” Darlene got it and started her own story.

“Well I was driving home one night, a couple of years ago now, loaded with groceries and we noticed a red sports car parked at the side of the road. Our place is not exactly on a major highway.” Sam had to know.

“Where’d you come from anyway?”

“California.” Sam gasped.

“A long drive!”

“His call was quite amazing, sad and apologetic at the same time, so we took and chance and, here we are; I thought he’d be alive when I got here, would have liked to have a word with him.“ Sam just nodded and waited while she calmed down, taking a few sips of wine, and continued.

“A man was standing looking under the hood of the car the way people do who have no idea what to look for but seem to think if you look in there long enough they’ll somehow spot it. We stopped, out our way strangers aren’t left at the side of the road. One of my boys was with me and liked the car. He figured out it was a clogged fuel filter, cleaned it out and got his car running again. It was late and I asked.

"Would you like to follow us and stay for dinner?" Emma thought, fatal mistake, she invited the raccoon into her nest. " He stayed the night and the next day asked if there was anything he could do to pay for his supper and lodging. Of course there was, lots, we produce our own food, but there's constant repairs to the buildings, grass cutting, gardening, it never stops. Long story short he stayed for the winter, no strings, never asked to share my bed, got along well with the kids, worked hard, and it was nice to have an adult around. We used to sit at the end of the day and drink wine, probably too much. We talked about everything; I asked him one night what he was doing out here, so far from home. He said,

"I'm just a lonesome sailor, on dry land for the winter, never stayed anywhere long enough to make a home. I'm like a minor character in a low budget road movie." Sam thought, that and the booze were two of his old trademarks.

"One day, out of the blue he asked. Darlene, could I stay past the winter?" She looked off in the distance, this part was painful.

"I agreed, thought he might hang in for the long run. My mistake, should have known better, had this kind of thing happen before, men don't stay too long. He stayed for about two more weeks, then one morning the Maserati was gone, no note, not a word of farewell." Emma was sympathetic.

"That's just not fair." Darlene smiled.

"Well no, but really what man wants to help look after seventeen kids that are not theirs? And sweetheart, a little advice from experience, never figure you can change a man, they come good or bad and stay one way." Emma nodded digesting the information, and she had come to know Pops, and was not even close to impressed. She had come to know Sam a bit and could see he came from much different stock than Pops, much more kind hearted and thoughtful, even though he was just a kid. She tried to comfort Darlene.

"He's done this kind of thing before, don't take it personally." She was curious. "Where did you get all the kids if they aren't yours?" She looked up at the deck and the kids were looking out at the marina and waved to her.

"They're strays, orphans, kids on the run, from group homes, foster care, abandoned, neglected, some abused. Girls especially don't do well out there on their own. Kids just show up, word of mouth, stay, for as long as they want. They're warm, dry, well fed and safe; they just have to pitch in help around the place." Sam said,

"You look after them, how long you been doing that?" Sam found that amazing and was also gathering information.

"About fifteen years, my husband died early, our place was a fishing camp. I didn't want to do that without him, too many drunks to deal with, so….here I am." This woman reminded him of someone else.

"You're an angel then." Sam didn't believe in heavenly angels but he always thought his grandmother was an earthly angel, always kind and patient and she always said to him when he left after a visit.

"Sammy, be a friend to the angels, the devils ain't worth the time." He could see the similarity between Darlene and his grandmother; he was formulating a plan based on that opinion.

Soon all Darlene's kids were bedded down safely for the night in some local cottages with an older kids in charge of several smaller ones. Darlene came back to the picnic table where the two kids were sitting looking out at the water.

"Well got them all bedded down, thank Tess for me will you." Sam said,

"Ok, let's do some business." Darlene was not sure what he meant.

"Business?"

"Pops had money Darlene, lots, and for reasons he only knows he put me in charge of spending it where I think it should go." She was looking more and more amazed.

"And?"

"You have an email address and a bank account?" She laughed.

"Oh yeah, not much in the account though."

"Well Pops has a lawyer and I've had a word with him; he is going to set you up as a registered charity and transfer money into your account as you need it." Now based on Pops recorded phone call she was hoping for something.

"Money?" Emma was listening closely, saying nothing wondering how much. Sam said,

"Over the next fifteen years, one million dollars." She grabbed his hands.

"What!"

"Yes, for what you've done and I'm sure are going to keep doing, you need money. Pops is making amends, let him, take his money, he don't need it." Darlene threw her arms around him and hugged him.

"You have no idea how amazing this is." Sam nodded.

"I think I do, but just a little bit." She hugged him again,

"Thank you so much; but I'm going to hit the hay, been quite a day." She left the two kids sitting on the picnic table looking at the water, Emma leaned close to Sam and whispered.

"Stand up." Sam did and she stood in front of him and took both his hands in hers.

"That was a wonderful thing you did today." Sam noticed something.

"Then why are you crying?" She just sighed,

"Because I'm a girl dopey, come here." Sam like all boys remained confused, but when a pretty girl says come here, you do. She reached around him and pulled him against her and gave him the best kiss she could come up with. She stopped for a second and whispered.

"You can put your arms around me too you know." He did what he was told and kissed her back. When she finally let him go she stood there smiling. Poor, or not so poor Sam was looking like a deer caught in the headlights. Emma asked.

"You ok?" He took a deep breath; he'd been holding it for awhile.

"Oh yeah, I'll be fine, wow, yeah very wow." Emma was pleased her first kiss had its desired effect.

"And you know what I want?" Sam of course like everything else had no idea what she might be thinking and he was still slightly stunned by the kiss. He finally said,

"What."

"A bowl of death by chocolate ice cream." Sam thought that was not one of several things he figured she might have in mind, but that was the least complicated. She grabbed his hand.

"Let's walk over the bridge." They walked over to where the adults were sitting around the fire. Sam's mom looked up, noticing.

"What's up Sam?"

“Could Emma and I take a walk over the bridge and get some ice cream?” His mom smiled.

“Sure, hey Emma, you keeping him in line.” She blushed just a little and said,

“He’s been quite good today Mr. Clarkson.” Sam’s mom and dad exchanged knowing glances. They knew something was going on for some time but decided to stay out of it. And on the personal side of Sam’s life they decided their son could look after that as well. His dad said,

“Sure Sam be back by eleven.” They wandered off and all the adults noticed they were hand in hand. Emma’s dad said the obvious,

“Looks like they’re buddies.” Tess smiled.

“That just seems to happen around here.”

Miss Bent Youth

The lesser Marginal Waters version of Trafalgar was approaching and the materials had been assembled for Eddy and Leah's boat. Robert was sitting in his deck chair sipping an afternoon whiskey, enjoying his relaxing role as tech consultant only. Leah asked,

"How many of these you built Robert?" He laughed trying to remember how many.

"Dozens, best design is a dory." Eddy added with newly discovered knowledge,

"Pointy at both ends." Now Robert was impressed.

"How do you know that?" Leah smiled.

"It's all on the Weeb, and we're smart." The voice of many cardboard yacht battles offered his advice.

"Good ok, triple cardboard on the bottom and sides, use rolled cardboard for ribs and seats. You know what ribs are?" Leah added with authority.

"Like people's ribs, gives the boat strength."

"Most impressive young lady and coat the outside and inside completely in tape, bare cardboard will soak up water in five minutes. When it's done I'll paint the name on it, be a proper yacht. Oh and tape a heavy cardboard triangle at the top of the bow and stern, strengthens the boat." Leah added researched information.

"They're called breasthooks aren't they." It was not a question. Robert held up his glass.

"Well said young lady and you are correct." With that they went to work and in one short afternoon the vessel was ready. Leah studied their completed craft.

"It's not very pretty." Robert added the voice of many cardboard boat sea battles.

"There's no style points in war." Eddy had given Robert the name that the kids had decided on and with their boat finished Robert set out to paint the name as given. In a former life he briefly painted boat names and graphics. With the job done he covered it in a cloth to keep the dust off. The kids arrived to check it out. Robert said,

"Ready and flipped off the cover." Leah looked.

"Who is Miss Bent Youth, me?" Eddy defended himself.

"I said Misspent Youth!" Robert blushed a little and put his hands up.

"Sorry, a bit deaf, thought that's what you said." Then added.

“It kind of fits though, boat should have a girl’s name and she is a little bent.” Leah scolded him.

“Hey, I’m not bent.” Robert just chuckled.

“Just, you know a little askew, it’s part of your charm.” Leah stood with her hands on her hips deciding whether to be offended about this then made the call.

“I like it, the boat’s named after me.” Like most girls not minding being the centre of attention once in a while.

Saturday arrived and the cardboard fleet was assembled ready for battle along with their young and motley crews. There were several different designs, some Robert noted wouldn’t float for five minutes, but Miss Bent Youth was in his opinion the pride of the fleet., heavily constructed, quite waterproof and reinforced with rolled cardboard ribs. His young boat building proteges had done well; he was confident it would serve them for the duration of the battle.

Three young boys put their boat in the water first and confidently stepped into it and promptly went right though the bottom; it sunk immediately. Tess under her umbrella sipping an afternoon iced tea, at least that’s what she said it was, made her first and easy call.

"Gunship is disqualified, crew get out of the water." The battle raged on for about an hour, some ships not lasting much longer than Gunship. But much laughter and splashing echoed around the marina basin. Adults assembled with afternoon beverages to cheer on their favourite crew. Soon there were only two left Miss Bent Youth and and the H.M.S. Victory, confidently named after Lord Nelson's historic boat and victory at Trafalgar. However the modern Victory was getting a little soft in the middle as its cardboard hull was soaking up water. Eddy noticed this and called to Leah.

"Let's ram it in the middle, full paddle power!" On either side of Miss Bent Youth the brother and sister team leaned on the paddles getting their little boat up to hull speed. Two older boys were the crew on Victory and stood helplessly as the better built Miss Spent Youth cut their boat clean in half. One of them yelled at Tess as their craft was sinking.

"They can't do that!" Tess who as the afternoon wore on had definitely switched to beer looked up and was feeling quite mellow but found a copy of her own rules, squinted through her sun glasses and made the call.

"Sorry boys, not a rule violation, you lose." Victory was anything but like its historic namesake, now in two picces settling into the harbour. Eddy and Leah held their nerf lances in victory.

"Yes!" However just then one of the boys in the forward half of Victory was not going down without a fight and took a hard swing at Leah hitting her in the head knocking her in the water. Now the win was in the bag but something in Eddy snapped, perhaps his primordial protective nature of family kicked in and he yelled.

"Nobody hits my sister." And hauled off and nailed the offending sailor sending him ass over tea kettle into the harbour. Eddy yelled.

"Now we have victory!" Tess who could generally be described as tough but fair made the call.

"Sorry Eddy you can't swing the lance, you just disqualified your team, we have no winner." Eddy looked around in dismay.

"Now what?" Now Pietro his uncle who had been cooking all afternoon made the sensible call.

"Let's eat!" With that all the soaked hulls were hauled out to dry in the sun to later be burned in viking funerals around the camp fire. Child sailors who had been doing battle a few minutes ago made friends, got dried off and like everyone else were fed and watered.

Geezers, woodpeckers and other assorted boaters, friends and relatives at Marginal Waters settled back, tummies full for an evening of drinking beer and swapping lies around the fire as one by one the tattered remains of the fleet were burned, except Miss Bent Youth which was still in good shape. Eddy and Leah couldn't bring themselves to burn their boat just yet, especially since it was accidentally named after Leah. Also they were formulating a plan; Miss Bent Youth would be taking another voyage, somewhere, somehow.

But for now they were gathered by the fire with the rest of Marginal Waters clan when Leah really surprised Eddy by leaning close and giving him a little kiss on the cheek. He made a little fuss.

"What'd you do that for?" Leah smiled.

"Thank you." Eddy asked.

"For what?"

"Looking out for me, that was nice." Eddy's eyes narrowed remembering.

“Nobody hits my sister.” Leah patted his hand.

“I know.”

The Call of the Wild

Sometime in the middle of the night Emma and Danny were woken up from a dead sleep. They sat bolt upright, both saying at the same time"

"What the heck is that!" Something, big, really big was running through the forest along the shore heading their way The shore was only twenty meters from their small island camp sight. They could hear a steady thump, thump, crash thump as whatever it was was getting closer. Whatever it was moving at a fairly good clip knocking down small saplings without breaking stride. Emma whispered.

"Is that a Sasquatch?" Danny whispered back.

"No idea," and reached for their only defence system, a flare pistol. He figured it had to be some kind of animal but really did not want to hurt whatever it was, just scare it off before it decided to run through their campsite. He held the gun up to the sky and fired. Both kids held their breaths as the flare went up and up then turned down lighting up the quiet lagoon they were in with an eerie reddish glow. The creature looked up; they were hoping it didn't have the body of a nearby camper in its jaws, but at the edge of the water was a huge bull moose. This is a large animal especially at close range. He had just pulled his head out of the water with about a bushel of water weeds in his mouth. At his full height he looked imposing as his rack must have been almost three meters across. Completely surprised and apparently alarmed by the pop of the flare pistol and that daylight had suddenly arrived. He dropped his mouthful of weeds, let go a huge sneeze firing a wad of partly chewed weeds out his nose, shook his head, snorted then turned trotted off into the woods, trailing a long loud fart behind him. By the time the flare hissed out on the water the moose was gone, obviously looking far a quieter weed bed for a midnight snack. Emma whispered,

"That was a good idea Danny, good thing we camped on an island too." He noticed she was shivering.

"You ok?" She nodded but still shivering.

"I'm ok, but it's a little cold and it's scary out here." He felt the same but didn't want to say too much and was starting to realize maybe his idea to run away wasn't such a good one, and agreed with her.

"A bit." Then out of the blue she said,

"Zip the sleeping bags together." Danny's eyes got wide. Emma's eyes were getting wet. "I'm cold and scared and I don't want to be by myself." Danny started to do as he was told but had to ask.

"We're not talking about sex are we?" Emma eyes got really wide.

"No, I, we can't…" Then she put her face in her hands and started to cry. Danny went into immediate damage control most distressed that he'd upset her.

"No Emma I didn't mean that's what I wanted. I don't even know why I said it, sorry, sorry." He went to work arranging the ground blankets and bags in place, stirred the fire back to life and stood waiting for further instructions as Emma calmed down. He patted the bags.

"There all good."

Emma crawled in and curled up. Danny thought it best to wait for further instructions. She realized he was waiting.

"Come on get in with me, sorry I'm such a mess." Danny was realizing there was now a lot more to this trip than he figured, and decided it was probably best just to go with it. He climbed in and lay on his side, waiting, finally whispered.

"I would never do anything to hurt you, ever." She wriggled back against him and sighed,

"I know, ok, bygones, but I'm still cold, need a cuddle, put your right arm around my waist." He did. She laughed. "This is a little funny, don't you think?" Danny agreed breathing a sigh of relief.

"Little bit." He was really glad the sex crisis was over then leaned and whispered in her ear. "Girls are weird." She ignored him and added another instruction.

"Ok, put your other arm under my neck." He did what he was told but left his arm flat in front of her. She sighed again. "Now bring your hands together and hug me a bit." He brought his hands together in front of her waist, as instructed. She looked back at him.

"There you go, gosh it's a good thing I'm here, you wouldn't know what to do." He thought, that is completely true. She lay there for a minute then whispered as she snuggled closer to him. "A little tighter please." He laughed, obviously a lot more nervous than Emma about all this and realizing what she said was true.

"I still don't know what to do." She let out a sigh.

"You're doing fine, now I'm warm, you ok?" He thought, if you asked me if I'd be sharing a sleeping bag with

Emma or any girl this soon he'd say you are completely crazy. He gave her a little hug.

"I'm fine, sorry again I upset you." She just squeezed his hand.

"No worries." Danny felt much better now that Emma was ok and just lay there for a minute and looked around; the woods was now dead quiet, the water black flat calm. It was well past midnight and the full moon's reflection was on the water and looked like the moon was just floating there like a shiny frisbee. It was too soon for evening crickets and Mr. Moose and all other animals were either asleep or prowling around somewhere else. Then he noticed things were really quiet, but Emma was still and breathing steadily. He leaned over her shoulder and looked, her eyes were closed. He couldn't believe it. He whispered to himself.

"She's asleep, already." Ok he thought, this is something new, he had to admit, it was kind of nice. Her little body was warm as toast now, kind of like cuddling with a girl sized warm teddy bear. He could smell her hair, thinking, she smells nice too, ok enough of that. He was starting to catch on why this activity was so popular.

Everything had quieted down, the wandering moose was gone and Emma feeling better, Danny also realized he felt better because Emma was now ok. He really didn't like it when she was crying and knew he was feeling more protective of her, though not sure why.

He also knew his plan for them to run for the summer was not going to work out. He wondered what it would be like to spend a day in the rain, then crawl into a wet sleeping bag; they needed plan 'B' which was currently unavailable. He took one more look to make sure Emma was ok and said to himself.

"I'll work on plan 'B' tomorrow."

Where the Heck Can They Be!

Both sets of parents were gathered at the end of the dock, they'd been in a major panic since they got up and realized both their kids were gone. The marina had been searched and all their friends had been called, no leads no luck. Tom had come around and realized immediately their canoe was gone. When he saw that he called Bill, his Coast Guard friend. With kids missing he arrived in no time, pulling up to the dock with his Coast Guard boat and crew.

Both sets of parents were still in melt down mode waiting on the dock as Bill arrived; he of course knew everybody.

"Afternoon folks." He pulled up a chair and got right to it. "Well what do we know?" Emma's mom was just holding it together.

"Their canoe and camping stuff is gone, so, I guess..." She didn't want to say it, more than a little guilt was circulating among both sets of parents. Bill filled in the obvious.

"They ran," then smiled, trying to lighten the mood. "At least moving slowly," and to give them some reason to feel positive, "they're both water rats so safer than most and the weather is good." He looked at the assembled parents and didn't want to ask if they had any ideas why but had to. "Any ideas why?" Danny's dad said,

"Both families are splitting up; we know the kids aren't happy." Bill did not know the back story, he found it odd that both families were coming apart at the same time and wondered what the odds and logistics of that would be.

"Both?" He was studying the body language of both sets of parents and figured correctly they didn't feel like sharing the details and it really didn't matter; the kids had to be found, that's all there was left to this story. Tom was there and figured since he wasn't personally involved would be more interested in talking.

"Where you think they went Tommy?"

"North into the system, lots of back bays and channels, maybe a cottage to hole up in." Bill nodded in agreement.

"Ok, I'll make some calls, put people on the lookout and we'll head up that way; we'll find them."

Meanwhile back at the kids campsite, breakfast was done and the canoe packed. Danny needed to know.

"Emma you want to go home, head back?" She had been thinking about nothing else since she woke up. Her answer surprised him.

"No not yet, got an idea, my Grandparents have a cottage on the Severn River; they're on a road trip and I know where the key is, we could stay there tonight." Danny asked.

"Would they mind?"

"Don't think so, and they ain't there so...." So the modern day not at all violent version of Bonnie and Clyde set sail for the Severn River, both not ready to head home hat in hand but not ready for another night camping with a bull moose at the water's edge.

They made it to the cottage easily by early afternoon, found the key and were settled on the dock as the dinner hour approached, when from around the corner came the Coast Guard boat with Captain Bill in charge. Danny rolled his eyes; he knew their little runaway trip was over. Bill called,

"What's going on kids?" As he stepped out of the boat onto the dock. Emma just shrugged.

"It's my Grandparent's cottage we're just sitting." Bill asked,

"They around?" She shook her head as Bill pulled up a chair. "You guys ok?" The kids just at there, so finally Bill just said,

"I got to take you back." Danny knew they had to go back and offered.

"We could paddle back." Bill shook his head.

"I got to take you, we'll put your canoe in the back."

So the kids had a quiet ride back to the marina thinking about what was coming next. And long before they were ready they sat facing both sets of parents. Both mothers were in tears but Danny and Emma were not; they'd been through that part and were now at the hardened stage.

Emma's mom agreed to do the heavy lifting and started.

"Kids we know you're upset." Emma rolled her eyes in a way that only a teenage girl can. "Emma just relax and let me finish. Firstly we're buying a duplex. We will live on the top floor and Danny on the bottom; you'll have your own rooms no travelling back and forth. Emma shrugged, deliberately trying to stir up a fuss.

"We don't need our own rooms you know; Danny and I have slept together already." Now if you really want to get the attention of a group of related adults and you're a couple of underage kids, just say that, actually don't. The dock went dead silent until Emma's mom almost screamed.

"What!" Emma spoke up fairly quickly figuring her dad would take a run at Danny.

"I was cold and scared, we just zipped the sleeping bags together, nothing happened." Now that was mostly true but Emma figured it was best not to mention the fact that she slept in Danny's arms and found nothing wrong with it at all. Emma and Danny's moms gave a huge sigh; they didn't need that on top of everything else. Emma's mom asked,

"So, ok to continue, or you got other news?" Emma just gave the slightest smirk and a nonchalant shrug again in a way only teenage girls can do. From the lack of other comments, it appeared that it was safe to continue.

"Guys, I know this doesn't make any sense to you, us either sometimes but our families can still work, you don't have to change schools, we're going to keep our boats and would it bother you if we all ate dinner together like we used to at the marina but now in the same house?" She paused for a minute. "We're going to go for a walk, think about it."

They left the kids sitting on the dock. Emma nudged Danny.

"How about then apples?" Now they both had a pretty clear understanding of the situation and how little power they had as kids.

"It don't sound too bad. Emma agreed,

"Could be a lot worse, could be on opposite sides of the city, new schools, no marina."

And so the box of gerbils got organized and as Emma said it could have been a whole lot worse, often is.

Slippery and Shifty Come For a Late Supper

The book so far has been like the others; it has a main theme more or less surrounded by an eclectic collection of other stories. Most of the main characters are children with a few adults thrown in such as Pops, the two legged raccoon. Now speaking of raccoons, that is the four legged ones, we also have to talk a bit about the animals that inhabit the marina. If you've ever watched otters play, they often seem childlike so I include them in with the brats.

Though the area is not pristine wilderness there is an amazing amount of wildlife sharing the same space and for the most part blending in quite well in the community, such as stoner Gordon mentioned in volume one. Most get along quite well with the humans but some can be a pain, but in their defence it was originally and still is their turf. They were here long before us and people tell us if we aren't careful may be here long after we are gone, another story.

This story I heard around the campfire and will relate it to you pretty much as told, more or less. Memory lapses and embellishment may or may not be a factor. Whether it's completely true or not, well you decide. The original author insists it is true but you never really know as drinking beer/ rum/whiskey and swapping lies is the cornerstone of marina social life. Embellishments are done and reality is often skewed by time and alcohol and in the end if no one is harmed what does it matter if a little creative fiction enters the picture especially if it leads to a good laugh.

As mentioned, Marginal Waters has around it an amazing number of animals. I have mentioned Gordon the groundhog and his family; they continue to get fat and giggly on what appears to be grass clippings and clover. Gordon has well recovered from his massive overdose of weed. Magoo and No Show have wisely found a new location to hide their pot other than in Gordon's underground palace. Where, don't ask, don't tell and it will all be legal soon anyway.

Another animal native to Marginal Waters is the red squirrel who are inquisitive and amazingly agile and will hop on a boat and invite themselves to whatever they can find or steal. One boater reports she was making a sandwich when one of them scampered through the galley, grabbed a slice of bread and dragged it off for its afternoon snack. Also having the nerve to sit on her deck while eating his stolen lunch. We have huge snapping turtles which cheerfully eat anything found on the bottom. I have personally fed them many chicken wing bones; they appear to grind them up into nothing and like most natural creatures are no harm to people at all. On days when I don't have chicken wings and there are a few, I swear the next day that turtle surfaces and gives me a dirty look. If he could talk he or she, don't really know would say.

"Where the hell is my breakfast?"

Also mink and otters, both quite happy living under the dock are quick and smart, very difficult to trap and why bother, a little live and let live is always good.

However nothing can compare to Slippery and Shifty, two legendary raccoons that have inhabited Marginal Waters for as long as I have been around, perhaps they are immortal! Or more than likely the current ones are the direct decedents of the original Shifty and Slippery. Their superior genetic material passed down to their progeny.

I believe the smaller one, Slippery is the brains of the operation, being female and in my dealings with raccoons always seem significantly brighter than their male partners. Ladies no extrapolations of the theory to your own partners or my complete gender. What am I saying, no woman has ever done what I asked to the point where I don't even try anymore. In my art classes I regularly get bossed around by nine year old girls, moving on.

Shifty and Slippery were legendary scroungers around the marina like most thieves, always working under the cover of darkness, devious and unreliable. No bag of garbage or loose garbage can lid was left unattended, however they were far more clever than the average raccoon. These are second story raccoons graduating several times to status of B&E artists, showing determination agility and creativity. But then again like us they have opposable thumbs, so could they be our genetic forefathers and mothers? It might be worth a government grant to investigate, Kathleen, what do you think? Slippery and Shifty case number one we just call:

The Zipper Incident

Late one night one of the skid row geezers who will remain nameless with the usual geezer issue of having to pee every two hours was up and noticed two raccoons (the aforementioned Slippery and Shifty) prowling around his back deck, as he had not put in the screens. He had dealt with many raccoons and knew them all to be up to no good. He watched with extreme interest since he could view the back deck from his peeing headquarters and had lots of time as peeing for geezers is hardly splash and go.

They found his cooler on the back deck, but he figured, all was well, it was well latched. They climbed around it poking and picking. He stared in amazement as they fiddled with the latch until, pop, it was opened. They flipped the lid then disappeared into the cooler and emerged with the contents, (the inventory was well documented), a can of sardines, I guess to be opened later, good sized wedge of Gouda cheese. That alone would inherit them a hail of shotgun pellets if I caught them on my boat, and that is, if I had a shotgun. They also made off with a white salad plate, and two small forks. Maybe they were planning a late night candle light dinner. Perhaps they have their own candles. The geezer watched in amazement as his cooler was selectively cleaned out. The horror, he stormed and crabbed the next morning, barely able to get down his free coffee. He rambled on at Tess and Tommy.

"Something should be done, the vermin are taking over the marina!" I demand compensation; it was gourmet tuna!" Tess asked what she figured was a good question.

"Why didn't you just yell at them and scare them off?" He flustered.

"I feared for my life; there were two of them." Tess just rolled her eyes that had already glazed over and walked away, Tom developed a case of the mysterious shrinking bladder. The geezer was left to his own resources. In his view vengeance is a dish best served right now. He thought about waiting for the vermin with a firearm but remembered in his early days some nut bar figured snapping turtles would drag down one of his stupid dogs that swam in the basin and shot a turtle in the marina basin. Nick the original owner hauled the man onto his boat untied the lines and said,

“Get the fuck out of here.” Since Tess was the original owner’s daughter he thought, you know, apple, tree and experienced had shown the residents that apple had not fallen far from the tree. Tess was not to be messed with, so plan B was formulated, not involving firearms.

The next night the geezer was prepared with a less violent plan. The cooler had been restocked, latched and the lid tied shut with a stout dock line tied in a none slip reef knot. All was well, he bedded down, sleeping the sleep of the prepared, that is until he had to pee two hours later. Up he got and there they were, same raccoons, same cooler, proving again what goes around comes around. This time the cooler was significantly re-enforced, so he stood watching, his reluctant penis in hand from the high ground of the superior species. His cooler lid was latched and tied. But it couldn’t be, he stood in amazement as one fiddled with the latch and the other chewed on the dock line. In no time the lid sprung open. He stood frozen in his tracks mesmerized by the cunning of his enemies, like we would be if we were confronted by aliens. Soon his stash was gone, sardines, cheese; they honourably left the plate and forks behind. When the assembled geezers discussed this over the next morning’s coffee and came to the conclusion that raccoons were likely just being friends of the planet and washed last night's plate and forks in the lakes, pointing out they do have opposable thumbs.

The Geezer versus Shifty and Slippery, The Final Chapter (not)

Extreme threats require extreme measures so the geezer in question was ready. Not having a shotgun and realizing firearms were not the answer but still he was not going to be beaten again. The screens on the back deck were secure, the cooler was re-stocked and latched and tied down with some extra 3/8ths anchor chain, padlocked. He was not fucking around; the superior species would prevail; Slippery and Shifty had met their match. Up later for his usual two a.m. pee he stood smiling as the aforementioned partners in crime were ambling down the dock; they had a plan, stopping at their usual spot both up on hind legs looking for a way in. It couldn't be, Slippery examined the zipper, poking and sniffing; she seemed to be perplexed. Finally finished peeing the geezer pulled up a chair; he needed to get comfortable to witness his victory. He had just settle down with a grunt when to his shock and amazement (I'm not kidding this is how it was related to me, though some of the details could be bullshit), Slippery reached out one long pointy finger, claw, whatever they are called and hooked it into the zipper and like she had done it a thousand times (maybe she had) unzipped the zipper. She and her partner in crime climbed in and went to work on the cooler, easily snapping open the latch. The chain was another story, even the combined intellect of Order of the Raccoon could not defeat the lock. The geezer remained fascinated watching them look around, could they be searching for the key? Suddenly they appeared to realize looking for the key was hopeless and started tugging on the chain. The plan appeared to be to pull it off the cooler and go for their third evening meal of sardines and cheese. The geezer lost it, there was no way he was swinging at the third strike, defeated by animals with brains the size of a walnuts. Fortunately having no shotgun he grabbed the only weapon that fell to hand, a fly swatter and pushed open the salon door to the back deck and stormed, i.e. limped up to the back deck. He screamed.

"Get the fuck out of here!" Well even the so called inferior species knows when it is out gunned. Not wanted to confront their larger and angry enemy, and like most of nature's creatures, just turn and run when encountering humans, bolted for the back of the boat. They did not take the time to open the screen, simply blew right through the screen, leaving two large holes in the back deck screen and splashed into the marina basin. Fortunately Slippery and Slippery could swim with the dolphins having leapt off many a boat to avoid angry owners simply splashed down and as the geezer noted, headed for the far end of the marina fast enough to generate a small wake. Two prime examples of The Order of the Raccoon were beaten for to-night but the war was far from over. Maybe they will return with lock picking tools? That would be another story.

The Last Case (Back to the Humans)

As summer wound down Sam and Emma had gone through all the pictures in the notebook and like Pops predicted everyone got in touch with Sam and not surprisingly none of them too much good to say about him. However their world view improved greatly when Sam e-transferred them some money to in some way make up for Pops' shortcomings. The kids had done well and when their parents found out after all was done they were extremely proud.

But there was one left and Sam was not looking foreword to dealing with his grandmother on such a personal level. He knew why his grandmother had not gotten in touch with him yet because he was sure she would have gotten the call like the rest of the women in the book. He had been around her and had overheard conversations about her; and nothing personal was ever discussed. He wondered that in spite of the call she might just let the whole thing blow over rather than expose her personal life to her grandson. Sam did not want the whole thing to blow over though he had no idea how much money she had, her lifestyle was fairly simple so he guessed she wasn't rolling in money. He figured a visit would be necessary; he also wanted to take his wing girl. She had been a big help with all this, being a girl had good ideas how to talk to women and was handy and energetic around the boat. And as an added bonus gave him his first kiss, which left him a little lightheaded. He was eagerly awaiting another one.

They stood a little nervously at grandmother's front door, but he knew they would get a warm greeting.

"Hello Sammy." She grabbed him and gave him a big hug and noticed immediately he was not alone. "And who is this lovely little girl?"

"Grandma this is Emma, my girlfriend." Grandma's eyebrows went up just a little then she gave Emma a hug as well and as usual had something kind to say.

"She must be a sweetheart then." Sam agreed.

"Yes she is." Emma blushed a little at this genuine compliment from boyfriend and his grandmother. She put her arm around his and Emma's shoulders and walked them in.

"Well come on in then, let's sit out on the back deck." They walked through the house Sam had been in at least a hundred times; his grandmother enthusiastically babysat Sam when he was that age. All his memories of her were good, lots of fun, stories being read and good food. She played games with him for hours and often took him fishing, one of her favourite pastimes. She was truly a perfect grandparent, loving him unconditionally and spoiling him a little before returning him to his parents.

They sat down and Grandma got down to business, but had some idea, news travels pretty freely in marinas and often in the area surrounding them. She had heard that the marina had quite a few visitors stopping where Sam and Emma were working. She had questioned his parents but although they suspected something thought it was time to let Sam deal with whatever this was and stay out of it unless asked. She smiled at Sam but knew that something was up.

“You’ve been busy this summer hon.” Sam answered honestly.

“Yes, it’s been fun and interesting.” Grandma smiled.

“What brings you by hon?” Sam took a breath.

“You must have heard from Pops grandma?” She stiffened a little and answered with as little information as she could.

“Yes.” Sam pointed out.

"You didn't come to see me." She leaned over and gave him a little hug.

"I'll make some tea." Sam knew that was her method of making some time to think; he'd seen that before. She left and Sam noticed Emma was looking at Sam's back. Sam noticed.

"What you doing?" She giggled.

"Checking to see if the sun is coming up behind you. Your grandma thinks you're wonderful." Sam just shrugged.

"I am wonderful." Emma nudged him and smiled.

"Not bad, do you like tea." Poor Sam whispered.

"No I hate it, can't bring myself to tell her." Soon grandma appeared with a tray with proper tea cups and a pot. She sat if down and they sat and looked at each other for a few minutes. Sam was nervous and it showed so finally his grandmother said,

"Sammy just say what you have to say?"

"How are you doing for money grandma?" She took some time to pour the tea to delay answering the question but finally said,

"I'm ok; why do you ask?" Sam took a deep breath; he knew small bits of his grandmother's back story with Pops because he was around for some of it, but really never paid much attention and stayed away from Pops cause he was usually grumpy and semi plastered.

"How long was Pops with you?" He knew this was really new ground for them. She took her time but finally said,

"Twelve years, on and off." Emma knew what that meant. Sam had one more question.

"Did he pay, rent or anything?" This was a tough question for a woman who was embarrassed by her whole relationship with Pops. She knew her family disapproved of him but had decided over the years and rightly so that her personal life was nobody's business. But still she often wondered why she put up with him and could come up with no conclusive reason other than it was better than being alone.

Sam wanted her to know that Pops had money, lots of it and and had spreading it around to the women he knew over his life.

He initially was going to show Grandma the book so that she could see she was one of the women Pops wanted to make amends to but Emma wisely said,

“Not a good idea to rub a woman’s nose in the fact that she had been cheated on, nine times!” Sam could see the sense in that and did not mention it. Emma never met Pops but had no use for him or anyone like him. Guys if you haven’t figured it out yet it is fairly common knowledge that women have no sense of humour for that kind of thing. Sam finally said,

“Grandma, I have dispersed most of Pop’s money and there is one hundred and sixty eight thousand dollars left in the fund; a cheque’s been written.” She went to speak and Sam just held up his hand; it was time to get firm because he knew what she would say.

“Grandma it’s done.” He handed her the cheque he had already had the lawyer write it. She looked at it for the longest time, then reached and hugged him.

“Thank you Sammy; this will be very helpful and greatly appreciated.”

With the last of their business done the two kids sat at Baby Bootlegger’s slip. The old girl had been completely restored and refinished and sparkled in the late afternoon sun. Sam noticed that Emma was looking a little down.

“What’s up?” She just shrugged.

"Nothing." Now Sam was starting to catch on about girls, nothing said that way was not nothing.

"Come on, something's bugging you."

"Well the summer is almost over," she paused, "I'm going to miss this, you." Sam didn't get it.

"Why, we'll be back for weekends." That didn't help.

"And after that?" Sam asked.

"What high school you going to?" She sniffed a little.

"Glendale."

"Me too, we can hang out there." Emma had not figured that.

"I thought you were from out of town."

"Nope, home town boy." He was catching on and moved closer putting his arm around her shoulder.

"You want to stick with me?" She rolled her eyes and rubbed the tears out of them.

"Yes, I do, sorry I'm such a girl sometimes." He gave her a little kiss.

"Yeah you are." She could tell it was not a criticism and she he brightened significantly now that the future was settled.

“This has been fun Sam; and we did good.” Sam nodded.

“As my grandmother would say, we were a friend to the angels.” Emma had noticed something about all the women.

“Weren’t all the women the same.” Sam agreed.

“Yep, gentle, kind hearted, and their kindness was used against them. Maybe Pops could sense that.” They both had grown up a bit this summer; learning other people’s stories, fixing up the old boat and an early introduction into light romance. Emma asked,

“So all Pop’s money is gone?” Sam nodded.

“Yep.”

“You didn’t keep any for yourself.” It wasn’t a question as Emma had kept the numbers in her head as Sam doled it out. Somehow to Sam it just didn’t seem right; the women Pops had wronged were the rightful recipients and it was Pop’s wish in the will. Sam pointed at Baby Bootlegger.

“All gone, except for the boat.” Emma asked.

“What you going to do with it.” Sam gave her unexpected news.

“I sold it already.” Emma was surprised.

"Didn't you want to keep it?"

"No, too young to run it anyway and it uses 100 octane aviation gas; it's about two dollars a litre, so, tough on my allowance.

Some guy from the states got in touch with Pop's lawyer, said it had been designed by his grandfather and had been trying to get Pops to sell it to him for years, no luck."

"So you sold it." She had to ask. "How much?" Sam smiled.

"You won't believe what he paid." Emma rolled her finger over. "Three hundred thousand dollars." Emma almost screamed.

"What! You're rich then." He smiled and handed her a cheque.

"We are rich." She took it and just stared at it then at him.

"Sam, get out! He just smiled. "You don't have to do that; it was left to you." Sam would have none of that.

"Nope, you worked all summer on it and really helped me decide what to do, we were a team, fifty-fifty." Emma just held the cheque and stared in disbelief.

"That's so so sweet, this will put me through university, come on stand up." Sam did as he was told. "Kiss time." They kissed and she hugged him for quite a while; Sam was discovering why this activity was so popular. She whispered, "It's been so good to get to know you." Sam whispered back,

"Me too, and as an added bonus we got another boat for next summer, come on." He held out his hand and she held onto it as they walked down the dock. "Oh and you know what Mary and her mom did with their money?" Emma just shrugged.

"They gave it to Kassi so she could finish medical school." Emma looked around as they walked.

"This place is alright." He gave her another look.

"Yeah, and here's the boat." They stopped at a slip and an old wooden runabout was sitting there, a little dusty, they could see needing a little t.l.c. but floating. "Jack gave it to us, next summer's project, if you want." She leaned in and gave him another kiss.

"I do."

Dear Reader,

You have got to the last in the series; at the moment it is a finished set. But you never know, things just seem to happen around the marina that turn into stories.

I sincerely hope you enjoyed the series and wish you…

Good sailing

Ron

Manufactured by Amazon.ca
Bolton, ON

13510496R00079